"This kiss changes everything, Shannie."

"What do you mean?" Shannie asked, sensing regret in Brand's voice.

"Oh, hell!" Brand released her then, looking at her with troubled eyes. "It means you're not just a friend's kid sister anymore. It means you're not just my landlady. It just makes everything different."

"It changes nothing, Brand," Shannie responded steadily, hoping to conceal the passions he'd aroused. "The house is large, and you needn't worry that I'll expect to be swept up into your arms every time we pass in the hall. As long as we both realize it was a mistake..."

"If I thought it was a mistake," he told her quietly, "I wouldn't be so damned concerned."

What was he saying? She wasn't born yesterday! He'd probably kissed a thousand women just like that!

Quinn Wilder, a Canadian writer, was born and raised in Calgary, but now lives in the Okanagan Valley away from the bustle of a city. She has had a variety of jobs, but her favorite pastime has always been writing. She graduated from the Southern Alberta Institute of Technology Journalism Arts program in 1979. Since then she has free-lanced, and her list of credits includes magazine articles, educational material, scripts, speeches and so on. Her first novel became a Harlequin, marking a high point in her career. She enjoys skiing and horseback riding.

Books by Quinn Wilder

Daughter of the Stars

Quinn Wilder

Harlequin Books

TORONTO • NEW YORK • LONDON
AMSTERDAM • PARIS • SYDNEY • HAMBURG
STOCKHOLM • ATHENS • TOKYO • MILAN

Original hardcover edition published in 1987
by Mills & Boon Limited

ISBN 0-373-02904-7

Harlequin Romance first edition April 1988

CHAPTER ONE

SHANNIE SMITH sat cross-legged on her living-room floor surrounded by perilously leaning stacks of magazines. With solemn ceremony she slid the final copy of *Kids' Corner* inside its mailing wrapper, and placed it cautiously on top of the nearest haphazard pile.

She ran a slim hand through a shining mane of shoulder-length, honey-streaked brown hair. From its faintly dishevelled appearance, the dark, heavy hair had obviously had a hand run through it several times already that morning. Her expression was unconsciously dour, and the huge, ash-coloured eyes that flicked from stack to stack reflected a bone-numbing weariness. Then a slow transformation began to take place. The weary expression dissolved into one of relief, and then of satisfaction, and suddenly Shannie's solemn features erupted into a look of sheer and gleeful delight that magically altered her countenance from pinched and decidedly school-marmish, to elfin: her features alive, laughter-filled, dancing with a slightly mischievous charm.

She stretched her slender frame mightily, brushed paper dust from a pair of blue jeans too faded to be much improved by the gesture, and then jumped to her feet, and leapt lithely out of her self-imposed prison of stacked magazines. Spontaneously, she broke into a mad and joyous freedom dance over the sparkling golden surface of the hardwood floor.

'It's done for another year,' she sang out to a boneless puddle of tan and white fur. 'We have the whole wonderful summer to ourselves, Snuggles.' She was regarded by two very unimpressed soft-suede eyes set in a pool of wrinkles above a flattened snout.

'Me and you in our inn for two,' Shannie warbled happily, immensely enjoying her private joke and managing to ignore the fact that her dog's eyes were now clenched tightly shut in a nearly human expression of long-suffering.

She jigged a step or two more, just to show Snuggles who was boss, and then with a contented sigh flopped on to her abundantly cushioned rose-tinted sectional sofa. She wrinkled her nose and stuck out her tongue at the magazines and then looked contrite.

'Sorry,' she murmured. Like many people who lived alone, Shannie had drifted into the habit of babbling away to herself, or addressing inanimate objects—like her magazines. Gravely, she continued her conversation with them. 'You do pay the bills. You allow me to indulge in this wonderful old place.'

Her eyes roamed around the high-ceilinged, french-windowed room, affectionately touching on the huge fieldstone fireplace and her treasured antiques. 'Actually,' she addressed the magazines again, 'I love you, too. I really do. It's just that by this time of year I need a break.' She sighed, crossed her arms over her chest, and regarded the artfully worked plaster of her ceiling thoughtfully. 'Next year,' she vowed, 'I'm going to hire someone to look after the mailing. I really am.'

She smiled ruefully. Chances were that by the time the September issue was off the presses she would be feeling refreshed and invigorated after an entire summer off, and she would once again take on the mailing herself. Somehow, though she was now making more money than she had ever imagined she would, she never seemed to have quite enough to cover all her planned projects. And the money she had saved last year by doing the mailing herself *had* allowed her to acquire the exquisitely restored Franklin woodburning stove that now graced her kitchen.

She looked again around the room, feeling warmed by its aged solidness. 'My folly,' she commented wryly, but without any real regret. 'You swallow money as fast I make it, don't you?'

Still, her smile was one of smug satisfaction. Because she did make money—a lot more money than her almost-career as a schoolteacher would have allowed. She was self-employed, owned her own home in the country, and was entirely independent—a situation made twice as delightful because of all the people who had warned her how foolish she was to even try and make a go of *Kids' Corner*.

The idea for the children's magazine, the

source of her success, had been born while she was a student teacher. She had noticed that many children were extremely talented and imaginative writers, and yet they weren't encouraged in any concrete, meaningful way. Maybe Shannie had been particularly sensitive to the problem because it was an echo from her own childhood. Her own talent for expressing herself with words had never earned her a trophy or her picture in the paper like a talent in athletics might have done. An essay brought home with an 'A' on it had never seemed to pack quite the punch of her brothers' rows upon rows of satiny ribbons and glittering trophies.

So, once a month, in *Kids' Corner*, Shannie had displayed the best of her class's writing in a highly professional format that she'd spent many exhausting, if loving, hours labouring over. She'd charged a modest amount for the magazine and issued small cheques to the successful writers. She confined her role to selection and layout only. The writing was by kids and for kids—and perhaps not too surprisingly, the kids loved it. The magazine expanded on its own—Shannie was soon receiving orders and submissions from other classes, and then from other schools and from community libraries. By the end of her stint as a student teacher she knew, from the boxes and boxes of mail she was sorting through, that she had stumbled on to something. She graduated from university, boldly left her teaching career behind, and became a small-time publisher.

She had never looked back. Her one regret was that she loved children and she had lost personal contact with them. On the other hand, she got hundreds of love letters from her loyal following. It was hard work, and yet so totally absorbing and rewarding that she seldom minded the great demands it made on her time and the great sacrifices required of her social life. Besides, she took two months off every summer, the same as 'her kids', and that was all she needed to recuperate and gather herself together. By September she would be itching to get back at it.

She had started three years ago. *Kids' Corner* now enjoyed a subscription list that numbered just over three thousand, and Shannie Smith enjoyed her old house in the Shuswap region of the British Columbia countryside, and the independence that her modest success had brought her. But just as important, she enjoyed knowing she was encouraging young talent—that her magazine had become the 'trophy' for youthful writers.

The phone rang, and Shannie gave herself a quick shake, realising how close to napping her contented musings had brought her. She'd been up most of the night getting the last issue ready for the mail.

'Hello,' she answered without much enthusiasm and a barely suppressed yawn.

'Goodness gracious, Shannie—I'd almost

swear you were sleeping! Were you sleeping?'

'Hello, Mother,' Shannie said, ignoring the question and rolling her eyes at Snuggles.

'What time is it there?' her mother demanded.

Shannie sighed. Her mother insisted on making it sound like half a world separated them, when in fact they lived only one time zone apart. 'It's an hour earlier here than it is there,' she explained patiently, though it was for about the millionth time.

'Hmmph. Then what on earth are you doing sleeping? Healthy, well adjusted people don't sleep at—Shannie, are you sick?'

Shannie registered the panicky note just in time to bite back her reply that she was at an age where she could choose for herself when she would sleep. 'Mom, I'm not sick. I'm perfectly all right. I was just up late with the last issue.'

'Oh—the magazine.' 'The magazine' was always said in exactly the same hurt, faintly accusing tone—as if it were a highway man who had heartlessly spirited away a beloved daughter.

'Mom, I wish you wouldn't worry about me. It's so silly. I am twenty-six years old.' Shannie felt that odd blend of exasperation and compassion that she always felt when she talked to her mother.

'A lot of good being twenty-six years old is going to do you when you're all alone in that monstrosity of a house and something happens and you need help——'

'I have the dog,' Shannie said with commendable restraint.

'The only possible protection that ridiculous dog might offer is if the intruder tripped over it and broke his neck.'

Insults to her dog aside, Shannie noted that vague fears were now becoming specific— 'something' had become 'the intruder' in mere seconds. In a few minutes, if the conversation was allowed to deteriorate that far—'the intruder' would have a knife at Shannie's throat while she screamed helplessly, with nobody for miles to hear——

'How's the weather in Edmonton, Mom?' Shannie made a hopeful attempt at changing the subject.

'Shannie,' the tone was petulant, 'don't you try to sidetrack me! You know how I worry about you being in that spooky old house all by yourself. I'll feel so much better when you're actually operating it as a bed and breakfast inn. And in fact——'

Shannie closed her eyes. She was beginning to suspect that one small lie was going to return to haunt her all the days of her life. Her parents— her entire family, brothers included—had been adamantly opposed to her buying the old house, mostly because they feared for her security, but also because they were hopelessly traditional and it just wasn't 'done' for a single woman to live alone, and especially not in the country.

Shannie had known, from long experience,

that she would never be able to make her family understand her—or the good feeling the house gave her—the love at first sight she had felt when she'd seen its sagging Victorian frame, the delicate gingerbread work around the porch, the shutter-framed windows that had looked to her like drowsy, friendly eyes.

Rather than taking on the impossible task of trying to make them understand, she had appeased them with an impulsive lie. Not even a lie, really, because at that point she had even considered, for a whimsical second or two, that she just *might* turn the place into a bed and breakfast. It *was* a big, rambling turn-of-the-century house—far too big for one person, and in her desperation she had convinced herself it might actually be fun running an old-fashioned inn as a sideline.

Shannie hadn't been able to kid herself for long. She had loved her new home—even its sad state of disrepair. She didn't feel the least bit nervous there by herself—she had faith in her newly acquired British bulldog puppy, even if her family had looked at him with ill-concealed dismay. The honest fact was that she was an intensely private person and she couldn't see herself sharing her quarters with strangers for dubious security and even more dubious profit, as her accountant had put it. Still, the myth of starting up an inn proved to be a useful one, and she hoped to hold her family at bay with elaborately detailed stories of the unexpected renovations that prevented the grand opening. Some day, surely, they would have simply grown accustomed to the idea of her living alone and the whole matter of Shannie Smith becoming the proprietor of an inn would fade, mercifully, from their memories.

A naïve wish, Shannie realised now, since two years had passed and, if anything, her mother was getting more persistent in her desire to see guests happily ensconced in her daughter's 'inn'.

'What did you say, Mom?' Her mother followed a rigid weekly format in her talks—a system that allowed Shannie to listen half-heartedly, if at all. It was at about the point in her call when she should have been lamenting Shannie's chances of ever finding a husband in the God-forsaken backwoods country of British Columbia, when suddenly Shannie realised her mother was not anywhere near the regular ten-minute marker in the weekly lecture.

'I said he needs a place right away and——'

'Who?' Shannie demanded grimly, giving herself a mental kick for her inattentiveness.

'Your first guest, dear,' her mother informed her, her voice radiating sweet pride at her good deed.

'No!' Shannie managed, biting back panic.

'But why ever not? I've just told you he doesn't mind if the house is a bit rough around the edges. He simply needs an out-of-the-way place to hide out so that——'

'No,' Shannie repeated firmly, not even giving

in to the temptation to ask if her 'first guest' was a
fugitive. Hide out? But even the slightest sign of
interest might encourage her mother to the point
of no return. 'I just don't have a room ready,' she
added.

'The room your father and I stayed in at
Christmas was lovely, Shannie, if a bit draughty,
and in the summer that shouldn't be a problem,
should it?'

'Mom. I'm going to finish the gable-room this
summer, so all the furniture in there will have to
be stored in the room you and Dad had.'

'Now, Shannie, that is not a *real* problem. Just
put that old junk in the cellar, for heaven's sake.'

Shannie clenched and unclenched her fist
three times in an effort to maintain her control.
She did not particularly appreciate a hundred-
year-old solid oak bed and matching wardrobe
being referred to as junk—even if they were
slightly scarred and a three-year-old with a
watercolour brush had once been let loose inside
the wardrobe.

'Mom, it's simply impossible. Rooms aside, I
need a rest. I was thinking of doing some
travelling this summer. I——'

'I've already told him he could.' The voice held
a vaguely triumphant note, as if that settled
everything.

'I beg your pardon?' Shannie asked coldly.

'Well, it's not as if he's a total stranger.' Her
mother was in wheedle mode now, and talking
fast. 'Ray's known him for years, and I think you

may have even met him. Yes, you did! Ray brought him home once for a few days at Easter break—the year he played university ball in the States.'

Shannie felt a shiver of pure dread run through her slim frame. 'Who?' she whispered.

'Brand Heaton. Do you remember him, dear?'

'Barely,' she lied coldly, and then gave herself a sharp mental shake. What was the matter with her? She had met Brand Heaton—briefly—years ago. She'd been a gauche and self-conscious sixteen-year-old. He'd been twenty-one—the number one draft choice of some pro-American football team. He'd refused to let her do an article about him for her school paper. To this day she didn't know why that scar ran so deep, and had hurt so much. She had cried in her room for three days over his insensitive rejection. The fact that his absolute aversion to publicity of any kind had never wavered—not for the reporters of *Time* or *People* or *Sports Weekend*—had never made her feel better.

She sighed. Even back then Brand Heaton's incredible speed, his almost instinctive skill on a football field, had made him big, big news. She had come across his picture more than once, and now she suspected that she had probably been nursing some secret and juvenile crush—along with the ardent wish that Brand Heaton would fall madly and helplessly in love with her. His cool and polite refusal to be interviewed had dashed her silly little notions with a vengeance.

And yet still, even being able to analyse the situation with ten years' perspective, she couldn't quite bring herself to forgive him. Never had been able to: she had watched his football career unfolding with a jaundiced and indifferent eye— if it was indifferent to mutter to a black and white photograph in the sports section of the newspaper, 'I hope your tight little pants split right open the next time you bend over, superstar.'

'Brand Heaton is not staying here,' Shannie said a trifle hotly, and then added hastily, 'and neither is anybody else. I'm simply not ready for it.'

'Shannie, you're being completely unreasonable. Now hang on a minute, your brother is right here, and he wants to talk to you.'

'Mother, I don't need to talk to ... oh, hello, Ray.'

There was some muffled conversation on the other end and then Ray spoke to her. 'I sent mother out to make coffee. I think we need to talk in private, Shannie.'

'The answer is no,' she said stubbornly.

'Shannie, I'm beginning to suspect that maybe you're not really planning on ever opening that place up as an inn.' The words were said with a cajoling sweetness—an invitation for confidences that didn't tempt Shannie for a minute.

'The answer is still no.'

'But what if I were to share my suspicions with Mom?'

'You're threatening me!' Shannie accused

blackly, a picture of her retired mother and father arriving on her doorstep to 'take care of her' crowding unhappily into her mind. They had hinted at such a plan at their Christmas trip—but she had managed to persuade them, once again using the 'inn', that it wasn't necessary, and that they wouldn't be happy away from their lifetime home in Edmonton—which was only too true.

'Sis, it just isn't a good idea for you to be living out there in that big white elephant, a million miles from civilisation, all by yourself.'

'I have the dog,' Shannie muttered.

'Oh, puh-leese! Rover is a dog. Snuggles is a . . . a thing!'

'The vet said Snuggles would be quite protective if the need ever arose,' Shannie told him defensively.

'Honey,' he said gently, 'your—er—animal, isn't quite all there. I'd just feel better knowing there was a man around the place.'

'Even a cripple?' Shannie shot back sarcastically, and was immediately ashamed of herself. 'I'm sorry.'

The picture she'd seen in last week's paper flashed back through her mind. Brand, frozen in black and white on a physiotherapist's table, his face streaming with tears of pain, his dark, almond-shaped eyes flashing white hot with rage at the photographer who'd broken in on the session. She had felt sick for him when she'd seen that picture—knowing how much he hated publicity, knowing how horrified he would be to find his pain plastered across the front pages of every paper in the country. It was the only sympathetic thought she had ever had for Brand Heaton, and it had been brief.

'What exactly is wrong with Brand?' she heard herself asking, striving for a cool note of indifference, and appalled with her interest.

'Didn't you watch the Superbowl?' her brother demanded, his tone faintly hurt.

'No, I didn't . . . the Superbowl? But that was months ago.' She had somehow assumed when she saw the newspaper photo that Brand's injury had been recent. Childish pride had not allowed her to show the least interest in the accompanying article. Now, for a second time, she felt a stab of sympathy for Brand Heaton that she didn't want to feel. 'Is he hurt that badly, Ray?'

'He's pretty racked up, sis.' The words were said with almost funeral-like solemnity—and Shannie felt herself bristling. Her brother certainly would not be above taking advantage of her soft heart, and her well documented reputation for gathering up wounded things—birds with broken wings, kittens with their ribs showing, and puppies with bruised souls.

'Look, Ray, I'm sorry he's racked up. I truly am. I don't much care for jocks——' she heard his yelp and sighed '——with the notable exception of my two brothers, but I still wouldn't wish pain and suffering on anyone. Still, I don't live far enough back in the woods not to have heard whispers of what Brand makes in a year. He can complete his recovery anywhere his little heart pleases.' She paused. 'The French Riviera is supposed to be nice at this time of year.'

'Shannie, that's what you aren't understanding! The man is internationally known—he's considered a star even by people who aren't football fans. He's—er—a bit of a sex symbol or something, and he's got enough on his mind right now without worrying about being recognised and having to hide behind dark glasses, and then having people barging into his most private life despite all the precautions he takes.'

'You want your little sister to live with a sex symbol?' Shannie retorted sweetly. 'Frankly, I'm shocked and surprised with you, Ray.'

'But he's not really one, Shannie. He's a decent, respectable, hard-working guy. It's the fact that he is so private that makes people so eager to know more about him—and leads the Press to try to exploit him. He sells papers, because he's a single guy who makes a lot of money and seems half-way decent, though the papers would kill to prove differently. Did you know some newspapers set up busty blondes to waylay him, throw their arms around him and kiss him? Because his picture sells papers but it's really hard to get any real dope on him?'

'Poor man,' Shannie said with saccharine sweetness.

'He really is a nice guy, Shannie.'

'Fine. Have him stay at your house.'

'My house doesn't purport to be an inn,' he reminded her.

'I just don't want guests right now, Ray.'

'Do you ever?'

Shannie was silent.

'I'm telling Mom,' he teased in a tone she remembered from childhood—and now, as then, she could hear an underlying threat, not at all disguised by the pretend playfulness.

She thought fast. What would it hurt to have Brand come and stay a few days? Suddenly she grinned to herself. It would be easy enough to make sure that was all he stayed: all she had to do was overcharge, serve poor food, provide no cleaning service, and, if it really came down to desperation, she could just call the local newspaper and tell them who her illustrious guest was. Perhaps she would even write the article herself—a retribution for his rejection ten years ago. She giggled.

'Shannie?' Ray asked suspiciously.

'I'm crying,' she told him sarcastically. 'I know when I'm well and truly beaten.'

'Good,' her brother commented with aggravating masculine satisfaction. 'Brand will be there on Monday.'

'Monday?' she squeaked.

'He's already on his way.'

'Pretty sure of yourself, aren't you, big brother?' she asked drily.

'Oh, I know how to handle the womenfolk,' he drawled with bluster.

'Gag. How does Helen put up with you?' We'll just see if you know how to handle the women-folk, Shannie vowed to herself. If she played her cards right she might still get the last laugh here. No oversized, dumb jock was getting the better of Shannie Smith. Not her brother Ray, and certainly not her brother's bosom buddy, Brand Heaton.

'I'll be waiting with bells on,' she told Ray sweetly.

'Shannie——' he said warily.

'Now I must go. Tell Mom I'm quite excited about the arrival of my first guest.'

'Shannie——' His voice was beginning to sound pleading.

'Oh, and one other thing, Ray, if you ever use the inn thing to blackmail me again, I'll call every paper in the country and tell them what the famous fleet-footed Stamp running back's real name is.'

'Shannie——' It was definitely a wail.

'Ta, Beauregard,' she said cheerfully, and firmly hung up the phone.

Shannie rearranged the cushions on the sofa for about the hundredth time, tossing them down to achieve just the right casual, comfy, carefree, I-don't-give-a-damn-if-Brand-Heaton-is-com-ing-here look.

She sighed. Ray had said Monday, hadn't he? Why hadn't she exercised control over her wicked little tongue long enough to find out a time? Now she was stuck all day waiting. She absolutely hated waiting. And she hated it even more when she absolutely knew she should not be waiting. She was acting as though star-struck, and she knew it. She was disgusted with herself. She had two brothers who played pro-ball. She had grown up around the inflated ego of athletes, and had always been mildly disdainful of people who admired—no, worshipped and held in awe—those who could catch or kick a football but not do a hell of a lot else.

In her experience, athletes were overpaid narcissists who had a criminally limited vision of the world, and their responsibility to it. This opinion—formed when she was thirteen and her oldest brother had entered professional sports—had been reinforced, rather than changed, by the regular trooping of her brother's friends through her parents modest three-bedroom bungalow in the suburbs of Edmonton.

Except once, she reminded herself. Once, she had been well and truly excited about the friend Ray was dragging home with him for the weekend. That friend had been Brand Heaton. She had thought, from having seen pictures of him, that he was going to be different, somehow. She'd thought she had glimpsed a depth and sensitivity in those deep, chocolate-brown eyes. She'd thought she had seen in the faint, upward quirk of that firm lip the ability to laugh at oneself and, more importantly, at the institute of football.

Now she realised that that was undoubtedly what most women thought they saw in him. Ray was wrong in attributing Brand's main attraction to the fact that he made himself unavailable to the Press and therefore a mystery. No, it was the look in those eyes—faintly laughing and yet also faintly lonely and vulnerable.

She knew it wasn't true. She had been on the receiving end of his athlete's cool hauteur.

Suddenly she saw it all again in her mind's eye. Ray and Brand were in the living-room watching a football game on television. She'd waited patiently for a break—so nervous she wondered if she would be able to speak. Finally she'd had her chance and, with her heart thudding and her palms sweating icily, she had managed to blurt out her question.

'Mr Heaton.' No, wrong. All wrong. 'Brand, can I interview you for the school paper?' The words came out in a rush that was nearly incomprehensible, and her cheeks were on fire when those wonderful, unfathomable eyes had turned towards her.

But somehow she had never even remotely considered the possibility that he would say no. Never. She had imagined sitting across the table from him, her pencil poised, asking sophisticated questions that would impress him immeasurably. She had imagined those eyes lighting with surprised admiration, imagined his husky laugh at her quick wit, even imagined that strong, tanned hand reaching across the table to brush an errant curl away from her prettily glowing face.

Instead he had looked up at her without a great deal of interest, said flatly that he didn't give interviews, and looked back to the game. And she had completed her own humiliation by bursting into tears and running from the room. She had locked herself in her room for the remainder of his stay, ignoring her mother's soft knocks, and creeping down the stairs at night to eat.

Anyway, her three-second encounter with Brand Heaton had been a long time ago. But she should know, better than anyone, that despite those awesome eyes that seemed to promise warmth, and depth and laughter, he was just another self-centred athlete.

So why did she feel this way now? Why did she feel not very much different from the way she had as a gauche girl of sixteen? Was she still nursing, at some deeply buried subconscious level, the juvenile and ardent wish that Brand Heaton was going to walk through that door and fall madly and helplessly in love with her?

She brushed an imaginary speck off her ice-blue silk trouser-suit—purchased, albeit defiantly, two days before—as just the sort of thing a successful magazine publisher who hadn't let success go to her head, like successful athletes often did, might wear.

My only motive is revenge, she told herself hotly.

'Miss Smith,' he was going to say with wonder, 'I hardly recognised you!' And then he would stammer out an invitation for her to join him for a romantic dinner for two in town.

She'd raise an exquisitely shaped eyebrow at him and smile kindly. 'I'm sorry,' she'd say with gentle amusement. 'I don't date athletes.' And then she would look back to the television with cool dismissal.

'Dammit,' Shannie mumbled. 'I don't have a television!'

Outside she heard the unmistakable sound of a car door slamming.

CHAPTER TWO

SHANNIE, with not a trace of the sophistication that might be suggested by a silk trouser-suit, peeped unabashedly through the eyelet curtain that covered the frosted oval window of her front door.

Maybe it wasn't him after all, she thought with a small frown. Surely Brand Heaton drove a Ferrari, or a top of the line Mercedes, or one of those cars with a name that sounded like a brand of spaghetti? What she could make out—through the holes in her hedge and her curtain—was a van. And not one of those playboy models with the smoked windows and sunset murals painted on the side panels, either. In fact, it looked like her plumber's van—a dull, utilitarian grey, with rusty fenders, an interesting assortment of little scrapes and dents, and a cracked windscreen.

And then through the lattice-work of leaves, she caught a glimpse of hair, and knew beyond a shadow of a doubt that it was him. No one else on earth had hair like that—a rich, deep brown, almost black, with each sparkling strand oddly silver-tipped. It was a phenomenon that was never really captured by pictures—she remembered being startled by it when she had first seen him in person—and she was startled again now. Startled and mesmerised by the way sunlight and

wind dancing across silver created an illusion of
liquid laughter.

She forced herself from the window with
abrupt self-censure at her whimsy, and settled
herself on the couch in a position of calm repose.
She picked up a magazine on refurbishing old
houses, opened it and studied a photo with avid
and unseeing interest. Suddenly, she decided a
Cosmo would have better projected the image she
was after, and then wondered wildly if a
magazine was even a good idea. Maybe it would
have been better if, at the sound of the bell, she
had come flying down the stairs as if she was
being dragged away from an immensely interesting project?

Too late to change her mind. She heard the
creak of the loose board in the bottom step, and
she puckered her brow in furious concentration
at the magazine. Nothing happened. She risked a
small peep up at the door. He was just standing
there. She could see his shadow through the lace,
but not his features. And, aggravatingly, she
knew he could see her. Was he spying? For God's
sake, why didn't he ring the bell like a normal
human being? Had he become weird in his old
age and infirmity?

Crossly, she tossed down her magazine and
went to the door. She did not bother to unfold
herself languidly as she had planned. She opened
the door—just as Brand was disappearing down
the path, back under the hedge arch.

At the sound of the door squeaking open he

turned his head and gave her the briefest of glances. 'Hi!'

She felt her breath threatening to leave her. Damn, if the man didn't radiate something—a raw power, gentled by the light that laughed in the depths of those faintly slanted, slightly exotic eyes. Even the voice, in a single word, had rumbled with a masculine mystery that went further than mere sexiness and made Shannie tingle like a schoolgirl catching a glimpse of her rock idol.

Flustered by a response she could describe only as disgustingly primal, she stared down at the two large suitcases and carry-all that had been deposited on her porch. How long was the man planning on staying? A year? He was coming back through the leafy archway with three more suitcases tucked under his arms. Two years?

She gave up her attempts to focus on the luggage, as those long legs moved into her range of vision. But she had expected grace, and was stunned that his limp was so noticeable—his left leg dragging painfully. Shannie found herself biting her lip—hard—to chase away the sudden sting behind her eyes. It was like seeing a piece of art that had been defaced. Her personal dislike aside, she had always admitted that Brand had a way of moving that bordered on magnificent— not that chest-thrown-forward swagger of some athletes, but something almost liquid—a way about him as smooth, as graceful, as powerful as water running soundlessly, forcefully over rock.

She forced her eyes away from his uneven gait,

knowing intuitively that her sympathy would not be appreciated. Lightning swift—in a blink he was sure not to notice—she let her eyes roam appreciatively over his body. It had a hard, lean look, as though it had been carved from marble. If his bad leg had forced him to be inactive it didn't show in the sculpted muscle that rippled in his chest and legs and arms. Nice muscles, she decided, sinewy and corded, but not bulging or beefy or brawny. A football player's heavily padded uniform could lead to all kinds of false expectations, but she noted his shoulders were naturally broad, tapering to a flat stomach and narrow hips. The strong, svelte frame looked natural enough, and yet she knew from long experience the kind of hours and work that went into building a body to that kind of perfection— and for once she was willing to appreciate the result rather than hold it in disdain.

Her eyes continued their journey and she found herself looking into his face. Brand's face could have never been called classically handsome. It was simply too rugged—his nose was too prominent and too oft broken, his cheekbones too angular, his chin too thrusting. It was an earthy face—the kind that could have belonged to a cowboy, or a logger, or a long-shoreman. No, his attraction—that mysterious, compelling quality sometimes called sex appeal—was more in the expression that could dance across the rugged, scarred surface of his face, than in either his finely honed body or in his looks. In his expressions, and in his eyes—those dark pools of light that seemed to hold a million moods, a million promises ...

Except at this moment the laughing mischief sometimes captured by a TV camera, the fierce intensity, the vitality and virility Brand Heaton usually exuded with such compelling force, were tempered. Even the eyes that usually glinted with the slightly mocking confidence of a riverboat gambler or an old-time adventure seeker, were not quite the same, though a hint of all that remained.

Mostly though, he looked drawn, the eyes shadowed with pain, the lines of his features chiselled even deeper than they had been. The set of his mouth was rigid—no upward quirk seemed about to erupt along its corners. In fact, in the strained line of that mouth, she saw his fight for control over the pain, thought she saw a lingering cry of agony not far from the surface.

Suddenly he was in front of her, the suitcases set down with a careless thud. She gazed up at him, surprised to discover all over again that, for a football player, he wasn't tall—probably an inch under six feet. She liked that—the brutish bigness of most football players had never appealed to her.

'Shannie Smith.' He gave her a tired smile, that didn't quite touch the dark surfaces of those pain-hollowed eyes, then studied her thoughtfully. Without warning the smile deepened devastatingly and then did flicker faintly in his eyes. 'You haven't changed a bit.'

Every bit of sympathy—every bit of that odd

kinship she had felt for him as he was coming up the path—left her with a *whoosh*. She felt just like sixteen again—and just as if he'd taken advantage of another opportunity to smash her confidence.

'I'm two inches taller, ten pounds lighter, and I no longer have pimples, freckles, or braces,' she informed him coldly, fuming. Oh, yes, the sooner she got rid of this ignorant cad, the better! Hadn't changed a bit, indeed!

Brand nodded solemnly at her correction, his eyes wandering over her face, and stopping for a long soul-searing moment on her eyes.

Shannie met his gaze and, though she managed an impassive expression, she was stunned anew by the depth of those eyes, the smouldering promise that seemed to be rising above the ashes of his pain ... she dropped her gaze hurriedly, confused by the wild stirring within her. OK, there was no denying that he was a very attractive male animal—but surely she had more control over herself at twenty-six than she had had ten years previously? Her confusion only firmed her resolve to be rid of this man as soon as possible.

'How long are you staying?' She commanded her voice to be businesslike, but it came out sharp and shrewish in her own ears.

His eyes were curious on her face, and then veiled. He shrugged. 'Why don't we just see how it goes?'

'Fine,' she agreed with cold satisfaction. *She* already knew exactly how it was going to go. Brand Heaton would be gone within a week and she could get on with her summer as planned.

She led him into the house, and to her surprise he set down the suitcases and ran an appreciative hand over the thick, carved mouldings of the door, and over the ledge of the wainscoting that lined the hall.

'Beautiful wood,' he commented, and she could have sworn his appreciation was real and not just polite. 'Mahogany. You don't see much of it around any more—not like this.' He nodded into her living-room. 'You've got some nice pieces in there, too.'

'Thank you.' Again she saw the warm appreciation in his eyes, and she could see his almost boyish desire to inspect the solid hand-carved end tables.

Her control slipped a bit, and she found herself offering, 'I try to collect early American pieces— just simple, well built pioneer furniture. I don't have much patience with anything fragile or prissy-looking. I don't even consider myself a serious collector,' she admitted, nodding at her very modern sofa. 'It's the spirit of the house that I'm interested in capturing and preserving, rather than the authentic details of the way it used to be.'

Suddenly she felt foolish for sharing that with him. It might be misconstrued as an apology for her modern pieces, and it certainly wasn't. Or he might see her as a nut—the spirit of the place, indeed!

Instead, he looked around the room and nodded solemnly. 'I think you've done a good job—this area does radiate something of the pioneer spirit—simplicity, warmth, strength.'

She momentarily forgot that her number one priority was to get rid of Mr Brand Heaton *tout de suite*. Instead, Shannie gave him her first genuine smile, thrilled at his perception—his easy articulation of the goals she had tried so hard to achieve with this house.

'What is that?' he asked incredulously, his eyes fastened on the cedar chest.

She followed his gaze and smiled ruefully at the trembling stub of a tail protruding from under the lid.

'That's my dog. He's a little bit afraid of people. Snuggles,' she called gently.

The lid creaked shut, then creaked open again—Shannie and Brand being regarded solemnly out of a small crack by a pair of frightened, dark eyes.

'How does he get in there?'

Shannie laughed softly. 'Snuggles can be quite ingenious when he sets his mind to it—which isn't often.'

At the sound of Shannie's laughter the lid creaked open a bit higher, revealing the full, awesome ugliness of Snuggles's jowly face.

'Good God! With a face like that, you wouldn't think he'd be scared of anything. He's monstrously homely, isn't he?'

Any points Brand had gained through his enjoyment of her house and furniture were lost. She'd probably been taken in. No doubt his comments were the practised result of attending highbrow cocktail parties where he would be expected to say something clever and charming about his hostess's décor. He was probably a hopeless womaniser who knew instinctively how to worm his way into his unsuspecting victim's affections. Ha! Well, he might be able to play his games on the kind of floozy blondes who liked football stars, but he was dealing with something quite different here!

'Snuggles is a delightful dog,' Shannie bit out with icy defensiveness. 'Of course, people who are given to making judgements on the basis of surface appearances quite often miss that fact—just like they miss just about everything else that is important in life!'

'Pardon me,' Brand said drily. His features were absolutely dead-pan, but she was sure she saw the faintest glimmer of amusement in those pain-haunted eyes. His amusement, and the fact that she knew she had been unbearably sanctimonious only made her angrier.

'Why don't I show you your room?' she asked stiffly.

'Lead on,' he agreed.

She paused at the stairs and looked questioningly at him. 'Are these going to cause a problem?'

His face became grim, his eyes hooded. 'I'm sure I'll manage.'

'Because there is a room down here that we could——'

'I said I'd manage,' he cut her off sharply.

Shannie turned away from him, and rolled her eyes. The sooner Brand Heaton was out of her house and her life the better. Who needed a hypersensitive idiot with a huge ego around, anyway?

But once again his appreciation of the house was almost able to charm her into forgiving him. Was it just charm? Or did he really share something of her affection for relics from another age like this rambling 'white elephant' of a house?

She watched him pause on the landing before the stairs turned sharply. He looked out of the window, and she saw his big shoulders rise and fall. Could that be a sigh of contentment, just like the one she had sighed the first time she had paused on that landing? She had looked out of the double window—looked out over the tree-tops to see the blue of Shuswap Lake shimmering in the valley below—and had felt the most marvellous sense of coming home.

'Do any of the rooms upstairs have the same view?' he asked hopefully.

'Yes. Mine.'

'Any chance of trading?'

'Not on your life.'

He looked around the landing again, a small, whimsical smile playing across his face. For a moment, the pain and weariness vanished from his features and it was very easy to see how Brand Heaton had come to be drooled over and dreamed about by women who had only seen his picture in the paper or on the television set.

'We had a landing like this in the house I grew up in. They don't know how to build staircases

any more, do they? Now they're just narrow
steep things that use space economically and get
you from floor one to two—but do nothing to
make the trip interesting.'

Shannie stared at him. She had been in this
house for two years. Her parents had come. Her
brothers and their wives and assorted children
had come. Several friends had made weekend
trips out. And yet not one single person had
seemed to feel even an ounce of affinity with her
house. Everybody seemed to think she was crazy
for buying it, for living here. No one had admired
the mahogany wainscoting, run their fingers
with faint reverence along the polished wood of
the banister, paused on this landing and sighed a
contented sigh.

He looked up suddenly, and caught her staring
at him. She turned abruptly and continued up the
stairs. It would be very dangerous, Shannie
informed herself coolly, to start believing she had
anything at all in common with Brand Heaton.
She was reacting to him like this only out of her
isolation—it had been a long time since she had
talked to anyone who liked old houses as she did.
Well, no, that wasn't quite true—the Salmon
Arm Friends of History Society met here twice a
month, and they loved her house. Still, it was
quite different having a dozen women, with an
average age of seventy-two, share an interest with
you, from having an exceedingly attractive man
share an interest with you.

And that was where the danger lay, Shannie
told herself. He was a compelling animal, Brand

Heaton, a view she would be wise to remember she shared with a million other women. He would have his choice of literally thousands of adoring women, many of them models and movie stars. Why on earth would he be interested in a faintly eccentric, highly independent, small-time magazine publisher who chose to live far from the fast-lane life-style he had chosen for himself, and who didn't even like football, to boot?

Yes, the danger was that Brand was showing signs of being capable of being quite a charming companion. And she was showing all the signs of being as fatally attracted to him as she had been at sixteen. Age did not necessarily add up to wisdom. And living with Brand Heaton could very rapidly add up to a heartbreak if she did not watch herself. She could very easily read more into their seemingly shared interests than he intended. No, better to keep her distance—and better yet, to stick to Plan A and get rid of the man as quickly as she could.

She sighed. Were all women as foolish as she was? Intellectually, she had no patience with the kind of woman who fell for an attractive face and a gorgeous body. Celebrity groupies disgusted her. Besides, she knew from experience that athletes had enormous egos that demanded admiration, adoration and attention, and gave very little in return. Rationally, she knew she would have nothing—but nothing—in common with Brand Heaton at a deep and meaningful level. And yet here she was planning a strategy not to fall for him, when in truth she half suspected it was too late.

'What was that for?'

'What?' Shannie shot back, unconsciously glaring at him as though he were a convicted criminal.

'The big heartfelt sigh.'

'Did I sigh?' she asked incredulously.

He nodded firmly.

'It was probably a yawn.' She yawned again daintily, just to show him she wasn't overly impressed with his company, and then gestured to the open door of his room. 'That one's yours. I hope you find everything satisfactory.' She nodded curtly—a proper proprietor's nod—and brushed hurriedly by him.

'Shannie?'

She turned back and looked at him. 'Yes?'

'What does that stand for?'

'What?'

'Shannie.'

She wanted to dash down the hall and pummel him with her fists. It was going to be tough enough remaining indifferent to him, without him getting personal. Not that there was anything outrageously personal about the question, but there was something in his eyes that she couldn't quite fathom—but that seemed very personal all the same.

She regarded him suspiciously. Don't you start forcing your big virile self on me just because I happen to be all that's around, she warned him silently. She gave him a tight smile. 'Sorry, that information is highly classified.'

'I'll find out,' he promised her good-naturedly.

If you were going to be here long enough you just might, she informed him sweetly—and silently.

She turned away from him again, and then, despite the fact that she knew better—despite the fact that she didn't want to encourage familiarity—she turned back, unable to resist. 'And what does Brand stand for?'

'Ma'am,' he drawled, 'I believe it's something they do to cattle.'

A reluctant smile twitched at her lips. 'Dinner will be served around seven.' She hesitated. 'We're having turkey with all the trimmings.'

'My favourite,' he told her.

'We'll see about that,' she muttered to herself, but somehow she didn't feel nearly as satisfied with the little trick she was about to play as she had thought she would be.

Brand went into the room she had indicated, set down his luggage and shut the door. The rest could wait for a bit. He sank on to the big four-poster bed, absently massaging his leg. He liked the room. He could see out of the window from the high bed and, though the view wasn't as breathtaking as the one on the landing had been, it was nice and peaceful. A herd of black and white cattle dotted a vibrant green hillside. The sight was soothing to him, and he sensed in himself a deep yearning for the tranquillity and silence and simplicity of the country. He stopped massaging his leg, folded his arms behind his head and leaned back, looking at the ceiling. Yes, he had a feeling that this place was going to be just what he needed. Nobody was going to bother him here. It would be a perfect place to work.

He noticed the stencilled tulip border that ran around the tops of the walls, and studied it with interest. He was willing to bet it was hand-done. She had a way with things, he thought. A way he liked. It was almost scary the way her taste mirrored his.

He frowned a little. Shannie Smith. He hadn't thought he would remember her at all, and yet he had. As soon as he had seen those huge grey eyes he had remembered. Intoxicating eyes that lured and beckoned and laughed and wept, and held the entire universe within their bottomless depths. That was all he'd meant when he had said she hadn't changed a bit: that her eyes were the same wonderful pools of mystery that he had remembered in the brief glance into them that had left him so shaken he had looked hastily to the TV—somehow afraid of losing himself, of being captured ...

Brand's frown deepened. Should he tell her he was sorry about saying no to her all those years ago? Not that his answer could have been any different, but his way of telling her could have used a little more polish. He'd been stunned when she had run from the room, crying—somehow thinking she'd been older and more sophisticated than she was. Today she'd said she'd had braces and freckles and pimples, but he hadn't remembered that—just those eyes, those eyes filling with large tears ... Ray had dismissed the incident with a wave of his hand and a muttered, 'Shannie's just like that sometimes.'

It seemed in an instant that he had understood Shannie's whole life—understood how her sensitivity wouldn't be understood in this house of heroes, understood how her particular gifts would never have been allowed to shine. Shannie finished last—after two hulking brothers who made the front pages. He bet it hurt her. He also bet she would never say a word about it.

He had gone up to her room later, knocked tentatively on the door, wanting to explain. She hadn't answered, and in retrospect, he could see now what a boy he'd been. At twenty-one he hadn't had all the answers, either. Because suddenly he didn't know what he would say to her, and he wasn't so sure he understood her, and he wondered if her brothers would misinterpret it if they found him alone with her in her room. He hadn't knocked twice. And, in all honesty, he'd never thought of it, or her, again until he saw her an hour ago.

Mention it or not? She'd probably forgotten it, anyway. Why bring it up? But somehow he knew she hadn't forgotten.

Could an incident more than ten years old explain the intriguing jumps in mood she displayed? One minute she seemed warm and enthused and eager, the next remote and wary and defensive.

He smiled. She was still sensitive. Boy, she'd reacted as if he had attacked her personally when he'd made the comment about her dog. But that was OK. He liked sensitivity. It seemed to be a quality that was sadly lacking in his world. He was fed up to the teeth with the brittle hardness and the empty-headed phoniness that were all too common in his circles.

He grimaced and looked at his leg. Not that it was very likely he was going to be bothered with groupies and hard-nosed Press people for very much longer. He gave himself a swift mental kick. He couldn't afford that kind of defeatist attitude.

And for that matter he really didn't have the time or the inclination to start delving in to Shannie Smith's personality—no matter how intriguing.

Reluctantly he unzipped one of his suitcases and took a framed picture from it. He stared at it for a long time.

'Damn it, Kelly,' he finally whispered, his voice torn, 'I think you've asked too much of me.'

He put down the picture on the bed beside him and sighed. The exercise equipment would arrive tomorrow.

CHAPTER THREE

THE kitchen was Shannie's pride and joy—the only part of the house that had been completely refinished to her satisfaction. The other rooms got done in bits and pieces, as her time and money allowed. But the kitchen had been in such a depressing shambles when she'd arrived that she had called a contractor and to hell with the expense. She'd had the entire room gutted, and started from scratch.

The result was an area that sparkled with just the right combination of rustic country charm and gleaming twentieth century efficiency. Sunshine poured through the corner windows of the breakfast nook, and played across the red brick tiles of the floor. The red brick was picked up again in an original old hearth that had been uncovered under layers of gyp rock and paint and wallpaper. Copper pots hung from ceiling holders above an antique butcher block, and an eighty-year-old copper kettle graced the gleaming surface of her Franklin stove.

Shannie sat in the breakfast nook, now and then glancing warily at the closed kitchen door. She disliked closed doors, but she could hear Brand thumping around, bringing in his belongings, and she really didn't want him to peep in and find her thoroughly engrossed in a book rather than in cooking the homespun turkey dinner he'd been promised.

She heard him coming down the stairs again, clanked the pot on the table in front of her, and grinned heartily. All the right sound effects of someone hard at work. Too bad she couldn't conjure up the right smells! With a chuckle of devilish mirth she returned to her book.

At six-thirty the stove bell went off, and Shannie went to the fridge, removed two turkey TV dinners from the freezer, pulled them out of their boxes and stuffed them carelessly into the oven.

'With all the trimmings,' she murmured gleefully to herself. She debated setting the dining-room table with her best china and silverware and decided against it. Then it would be too obvious it was a joke—and she wanted Brand to think TV dinners were the regular fare around here. If he had a normal athletic obsession with health, he would take one look at those little tin compartments of compressed food and start packing his bags.

For a moment, Shannie felt a twinge of regret. In fact, earlier this afternoon she had actually considered running into town for a real turkey, a desire she recognised as a purely feminine inclination to win his approval—to gain the admiration she had yearned for, and even dreamily imagined in his eyes when she was sixteen. It was strange—she wasn't officially a feminist, but then again she certainly wasn't anybody's sweet little Dorothy Domestic, either. Where had this

strange longing come from, to see if the old
adage—that you could win a man through his
stomach—really worked?

Brand came down promptly at seven and,
when she saw his eyes light up as he gazed around
the kitchen, she again felt a twinge of regret. She
allowed herself to study him for a moment. He
looked less tired, and she felt a twinge of an
entirely different kind at the picture he cut in the
casual tawny-coloured sports shirt that moulded
to his broad shoulders, his carved outline, his flat
stomach——

'Have a seat at the breakfast nook,' she invited
quickly, ordering her eyes to explore no more of
that supple, so-inviting frame.

Fighting to keep a straight face, she turned
from him, pulled a dinner from the stove and
plopped it down in front of him. She had to fight
herself with everything she had not to burst out
laughing as the emotions played across his face:
first disbelief, then shock, then disappointment,
and finally disgust. Then again, she wasn't quite
sure if her desire to laugh was caused by genuine
mirth or a bad case of nerves.

She retrieved her own dinner from the oven,
and slid into place across the table from him.
Suddenly the dining-room did seem like a better
idea. It would have put more distance between
them, provided an atmosphere of decidedly cold
formality, removed her a few paces from his
unconscious but very animal magnetism. She
wondered frantically how to suggest moving
without seeming like a nut—how could she insist

they retire to the dining-room to eat TV dinners? She couldn't, she realised, her eyes glued on her plate. He was so terribly close to her that she had glimpsed the rings of gold that surrounded his brown eyes. If she wasn't careful, if she slipped for an instant, her knees would brush his under the table.

With effort, she tucked her legs under her chair, and took a tentative bite of her meal. 'Great,' she forced herself to say, looking up at him with a defiantly cheerful smile.

The disgust had faded from his face, and his eyes seemed to spark with a hidden amusement, though his features were impassive.

'Oh, all of my favourites,' he told her with not entirely unpleasant sarcasm, 'plastic turkey, synthetic cranberry sauce, "this-is-an-oil-by-product" mashed potatoes, shredded newspaper dressing, and all topped with cream of cardboard gravy—including Mom's home-made apple pie.' He started to eat. 'Oh, yum! I hope there's seconds,' he commented drily.

'Tomorrow we're having roast beef,' she told him brightly, 'with all the trimmings.'

'I think I see a small problem in paradise,' he muttered, stirring the contents of his tin absently.

The twinge of regret was becoming a rather large squeeze. Did he really think her house was that perfect—that he would call it paradise, even as absently as he had?

She struggled for a moment. She could have some of her nearly-famous Everything-Under-the-Sun stew ready in the microwave in less than ten minutes.

Wait a minute, Shannie, she reminded herself sternly, the whole point is for him not to like it here. Don't start feeling sorry for him because he has a dejected and starving look on his face. Drive home the final run.

She got up casually from the table, hoping he was engrossed enough in his own misery not to notice her barely touched meal. She slipped it into the bin and, with a deep breath, opened the drawer beside the fridge and removed a packet of cigarettes—left by somebody at the last Friends of History meeting.

With a sigh of what she hoped passed itself off as pure contentment, she resettled at the breakfast nook, took out a cigarette and inexpertly lit it. With admirable effort she didn't choke, though she could feel her blood retreating to her feet.

She smiled shakily at him. 'You don't mind if I smoke, do you?' she asked, striving for the husky tones of a 1940s platinum-blonde film star.

He glared at her, then reached behind him and shoved open the window. 'It's your lungs, life, heart and health,' he said grimly, watching her with narrowed eyes.

'And it is my house,' she pointed out defensively, taking a deep and defiant puff. She gave a constrained small cough or two. 'Smoker's hack,' she informed him.

He said nothing, continuing to watch her with a narrow gaze that was beginning to make her feel like an insect pinned to a card. Stubbornly she smoked the cigarette until it nearly burned her fingers.

'Why are you doing this?' he asked, when she finally stubbed it out.

'What?' Her eyes widened with innocence even as her heart pounded with guilt.

He looked faintly disappointed in her, which brought her pointed chin thrusting forward, even as she felt a rather overwhelming sense of self-shame.

'Shannie, this isn't a kitchen that belongs to somebody who cooks TV dinners.'

'Maybe the kitchen was like this when I bought the house,' she said, hoping the loudness of her voice would make up for its lack of conviction.

'Oh, I don't think so. I'm finding it pretty easy to tell where the old house leaves off and the Shannie house begins.'

She quelled the flush of pure pleasure which that offhand remark made her feel and continued to look at him expectantly.

'And people who smoke regularly don't smell sweet as spring flowers, Shannie.' Her ridiculous pleasure probably showed in cheeks that suddenly felt faintly feverish. 'And,' he continued, 'their houses usually have a lingering tobacco aroma. This house smells like hardwood and wax, fresh linen and summer.'

'Oh,' she said weakly.

'Oh?' he prodded, his eyes glittering with satisfaction.

'Are you planning on going into the private detective business some day?' she asked, evading the specifics. 'You're really unusually astute—for a football player.'

She watched his face harden and tried to feel a modicum of pleasure—after all, how likely was he to stay in a place where he was going to be insulted?

'You know,' he told her, his voice soft with irritation, 'if there's a myth I've come to despise, it's the one that athletes are all brawn and very little brain. The truth is that most sports require lightning-swift mental and physical reflexes. The truth is that football is a sophisticated game that leaves very little margin for stupidity. The truth is that every guy I play ball with has at least one university degree, and more than one of them holds a PhD.'

'Hmmm,' Shannie said unrepentantly. 'Doctorate of Basket-Weaving. Has a nice authoritative ring to it.'

'For God's sake, Shannie, neither of your brothers is a mental lightweight! I could see you subscribing to an unsubstantiated myth if you were like most of the general public and didn't know any better, but that's not the case.'

'I grant you Len and Ray both have good minds,' she agreed quietly and seriously. Now she wasn't just trying to get his goat. 'They breezed through university with the greatest of ease—taking Mickey Mouse courses, mind you, that wouldn't interfere too greatly with their real reason for being there—the almighty pigskin. Not an iota of their intelligence has ever gone into anything else—it's been used to learn every play and every statistic and every strategy that ever existed. Neither of them has ever "wasted" an ounce of his intellectual energy on anything outside of that narrow little world. Len told me he thought Amadeus was a kind of liqueur until he saw the movie. Ray wouldn't know who the leader of his province was—and couldn't care less, either.'

Brand's eyes had widened in astonishment at the vehemence of her speech, and she had the good grace to blush. 'I'm sorry,' she stammered. 'I didn't mean to go on like that. You touched a sensitive nerve.'

He whistled a low musical note. 'You're not kidding!' He was watching her with a keen perception that made her feel exceedingly uncomfortable—as if her mind was being unclothed. 'You can tell me about it, if it'll help. It couldn't have been easy for you growing up with two superstar brothers.'

To her horror she could feel tears stinging her eyes. It was the gentle concern in his voice as much as anything else that brought about the disproportionate reaction. She'd been intentionally mean to him, and he was still being nice. Maybe he'd changed from that snooty young schoolboy who had refused to let her do an interview ten years ago. Or maybe, even worse, she'd been in the wrong—a hypersensitive teenager—and he'd never been that way at all . . .

'Look, Brand, I'm not implying I'm not proud of my brothers, because I am. And I take back the insinuations I might have made about your intelligence. Now let's just drop the whole thing, OK?'

'You're going to tell me about it some day, Shannie,' he vowed softly. 'It's not good to keep that kind of pain locked up inside you.'

'Don't be silly,' she told him shakily. 'There isn't anything to tell, except the normal tales of sibling rivalries and petty jealousies. And even if there was something, why would I tell you? You're a perfect stranger.' But even as she said it she knew it wasn't quite true, or at least not as much as it should have been after such a short acquaintance. She felt an odd sense of knowing him—of having known him for a long, long time.

'Sometimes a perfect stranger is just the one to tell.'

His unthinking confirmation that they were indeed perfect strangers when she felt an inexplicable bond to him, reminded her of the danger of she and Brand feeling very different things for one another.

She shifted the conversation hurriedly away from the personal. 'I'm beginning to suspect *your* degree is in psychology,' she remarked lightly.

'Wrong. It's in Natural Substance Engineering and Architecture.'

She frowned, not wanting to show her ignorance—especially in light of the intellectual snobbery she had demonstrated a few minutes ago. But then, with a small, self-effacing smile, she surrendered to curiosity. 'What's that?'

'Well, it used to be called Basket-Weaving, but it got a bad rep as a Mickey Mouse course.'

She chuckled. 'OK. You got your shot. I deserved that.'

He smiled back, and she sensed again the sizzling danger posed by this man. It should be illegal to practise a smile that lethal in the presence of a single woman! It was the complete absence of leering wolfishness that made the smile so attractive—it was just open and boyish and warm—a slightly chipped eye tooth somehow just adding to the attractiveness, giving him so much more character than the cardboard-perfect figures who posed for cigarette and whisky ads, or who oozed machismo and shot off bullets at each other on evening television programmes.

Maybe that was also why he had a female fan club that probably numbered in the hundreds of thousands, she reminded herself sternly. Because he had none of that cool untouchability, none of that ice-cold bronzed-god perfection. There was no message of conceit in that blunt, earthy face, no unspoken warning of 'hands off—unless you can give Farrah Fawcett a run for her money'.

No, in that face was a kind of tough resiliency and honesty that didn't mask an underlying sensitivity. Brand Heaton, superstar, looked like what he was—a man. Every inch a man and yet simply a man. He looked approachable and, except for those extraordinary eyes, ordinary. He didn't give off the vibes of a man too full of himself, even after all these years of withstanding the demands of an adoring public.

That was what the women loved, Shannie told

herself, the fact that it was so easy to believe Brand Heaton could happen to you. And she had better remember the danger of that particular myth, because Brand Heaton, as yet, had not 'happened' to anyone. He had never been married. Not even engaged. If there had ever been a serious relationship in his life it was an event that had been missed by the persistent Press who dogged his footsteps despite, or maybe because of, his attempts to lead out his life in uninterrupted privacy.

Considering the fancy footwork she had done to get away from the personal, the next question that popped out of her mouth took her completely by surprise.

'How come you're not married, Brand?'

'Aw shucks, nobody ever asked.'

'I find that hard to believe,' she said drily.

'What's your interest? Ye gods, you sound just like my mother!'

'And like mine,' she admitted with wry self-mockery. 'I guess I just can very easily picture you bouncing babies on your knee.' Now she was getting too personal and she knew it—but it was true, she could see him blossoming in a family situation. And from the sudden aching, yearning emptiness she felt in her own breast, she was suddenly sorry she had brought it up.

'Shannie! I have an image to protect.'

'Ha!' Despite the lightness of his reply she had seen the flash of wistfulness darken his eyes, but she willingly followed his example and kept it light. To prod too deep or too hard might encourage him to reciprocate. 'You contributed nothing to creating your image in the first place.'

'Most people believe it, you know, Shannie. The whole playboy thing. Why don't you?'

'Because you'd have to have the strength of a lion, the stamina of an elephant, and the agility of a mountain goat to give credence to half the exploits the Press marks up to you.' She hesitated, the lightness leaving her voice. 'Maybe I did believe it. I just don't now. I bet anybody who talks to you for five minutes doesn't believe much of the hype any more.'

A strong hand closed over hers, and squeezed companionably. 'Thanks, Shannie. It's been a long time since anybody said anything that nice to me.' He withdrew his hand, and she felt an aching sense of loss. His hand around hers had felt so right, somehow—natural and solid and good.

A little red warning light was flashing on and off in her head. Danger—he definitely did have the gift of charm even if his playboy reputation had been blown totally out of the realm of believability.

Get up and do the dishes, she ordered herself. She looked around frantically. TV dinners did not leave large numbers of dishes.

'Would you like a coffee?' she asked desperately, pushing away from the table, and getting up with more jerky nervous energy than grace. 'To take up to your room?'

'Tired of my company?' he asked bluntly, and then stuck out his lower lip in a pretend pout.

'Of course not!' she snapped. 'I'm just sure you have better things to do than entertain me.'

'Am I being entertaining?' he asked with exaggerated delight. 'Actually, I have nothing better to do tonight than entertain a lovely lady.'

She rolled her eyes, and hoped *he* hadn't noticed her calmly spooning sugar into her coffee-maker.

'Tomorrow——' she turned at the odd weary note that had entered his voice, '——well, tomorrow it will be a different story.'

'Why?' she asked, striving to sound casual, though the change in his face concerned her. In a split second it had gone from teasing and lively, to world-weary and closed.

'Vacation's over,' he said crisply. 'My exercise equipment's arriving.'

'Oh.' It was all she could trust herself to say— when in actual fact she was burning to know what underlying sadness was involved in the arrival of his equipment—even to throw herself at him and beg him not to do this thing that promised to change him so much—take him from her as she knew him tonight and fling him back into a world she sensed was full of grim pain, and not much of anything else.

She wanted to ask him why it was so important, but sinkingly, she already knew—the almighty pigskin. She sighed. The game of football had mercilessly robbed her of affection and attention all her life. Why did it still surprise her when it took again more? Especially with Brand Heaton—his commitment to the pigskin was absolute. That was another thing about him that she'd do well not to forget.

'You know, I do want to get married some day,' he said, shifting back to their former conversation with an ease she found aggravating. 'It just never seemed fair to subject a wife to football. I'm married to my profession for six months of the year. It takes it all—I just don't have anything else to give. That's not fair to a wife—or to kids. I really love kids, but I don't want to be Dr Jekyll and Mr Hyde for them—six months of the year you're Daddy Wonderful, and the other six you're away half the time, and when you're not, you're so tired and hurting that you can't even play with them. And meanwhile the kids in school are more interested in your daddy's autograph than in you.' He shook his head. 'Nope. A celebrity parent wouldn't be that great for a family, I don't think.'

She refused to turn and look at him, knowing she had just paled. Was he doing this deliberately—acting on his vow to have her confide in him? If he added two brothers who'd followed in daddy's footsteps she would turn and throw the coffee grounds at him. But he added nothing, and she risked a peep at him. Was he really that thoughtful that he had looked ahead and seen what his career could do to a family? To a little girl, who had the talent and imagination to be a writer, and probably would have been if she had received one encouraging word?

'You sigh a lot,' he said.

'Do I?'

'Either that or the dog's under the table.'

'The dog's in the cedar chest.'

He nodded solemnly, and she knew her sensitivity on the subject of Snuggles had been noted. He didn't seen to be able to do anything, though, about the twitching of his lips.

'When does the dog come out of the chest?' he asked in admirably even tones.

'Probably when you leave. That's the way it was when my father was here. And my brothers. It's just men he reacts to like that. The vet thinks he was abused.'

A look of outraged fury darkened Brand's face. 'What kind of person does that to a helpless animal?'

She set down a coffee mug in front of him and studied him thoughtfully. 'What kind of person does that to himself?'

'What does that mean?' he asked with faint hostility.

'Why are you trying to go back to football, Brand? You're thirty-one years old. It's over. You're abusing yourself. You know you'll get hurt worse, you won't heal as fast. You said it takes it all for six months of the year—are you willing to give it the rest of your life? A game? Do you really want to live in constant pain for the rest of your days? That I don't understand. I don't always give Len and Ray credit for brains, but at least they know when to call it quits. Ray—who is younger than you—will be retiring at the end of the season. Len's been coaching for years.'

'Don't!' he commanded wearily. 'They all say

I'll never play again. The doctors. The reporters.
They don't understand. You don't understand. I
have to.'

He got up, the steaming coffee forgotten, and
limped away.

She stared after him sadly. She knew intuitively that she would not see Brand Heaton as he
had been tonight again for a long, long time. His
lonely struggle had started. He belonged to the
game—heart, body, mind and soul. And she
shouldn't care. Not this much. But she did.

CHAPTER FOUR

SHANNIE awoke with a start, fear clutching at her throat. She bolted up in bed, listening with growing horror to the noises coming from downstairs. A man was yelling. The dog was howling. Dishes were breaking. Her eyes raced to the clock as if the time might help her make some sense out of this—it didn't. It was six o'clock in the morning—the only time she ever saw six in the morning was when she came at it from the other way, having worked all night.

The bedlam downstairs seemed to be increasing in tempo—crashing pots and pans, the high scream of the blender. The blender? Taking a deep breath, she tossed back the quilt and hurried out of the door and down the stairs as if the very speed and decisiveness of her actions could convince her of her courage.

Taking another deep and steadying breath, she peered around the corner into the kitchen.

Brand Heaton stood at the counter, clad only in the briefest of navy blue silky running shorts. He was beating some concoction in a large bowl and bellowing at the top of his lungs. But what was truly amazing was that Snuggles was firmly entrenched beside him—his jowl pressed into Brand's hairy leg, his muzzle lifted in song, his stubby little tail thumping the floor joyously.

'Shut up!' Shannie commanded, pushing into the kitchen and standing behind them, foot tapping, hands on hips. 'Quiet!' she yelled when her first order was either lost among the noise or ignored.

The blender was flipped off. The beaters stopped whirring. Brand ceased his caterwauling, and Snuggles turned and gave her a reproachful look which clearly accused her of being a party pooper.

'What is going on?' she demanded.

Brand turned and favoured her with a lopsided grin, and then the grin faded and his eyes widened. 'Shannie,' he said in a hushed tone, 'you're not dressed!'

She glanced down at the too-large T-shirt that barely reached her thigh. Compared to what he was wearing she was practically in a nun's habit! She tried not to think about what he was wearing—or more accurately, not wearing. His skin was sun-burnished and satiny-textured and her fingers twitched with a desire to know the feeling of that spendidly muscled surface. She folded her arms firmly over her chest, refusing to be distracted from her mission.

'What is going on, for God's sake?'

Brand looked puzzled. 'I'm just fixing a little breakfast, Shannie.' As if to prove it, he rushed over to the stove, flipped some pancakes, and then rushed back to the counter and poured the mix from the bowl in front of him into a frying pan.

'But is all that noise really necessary?' she asked grouchily.

'I was quiet when I was in the shower,' he told her, obviously expecting high praise for this huge effort. When none was forthcoming, he looked at her, his expression wounded.

'And it wasn't noise—it was singing.' He brought his frying pan over to the stove. 'Time you were up, anyway. The day's half over.'

'Singing?' she declared a little shrilly. 'Half over?' She wondered how much of that shrill note had to do with the broad, bronzed back that had been presented to her—the muscles in it rippling with his every move. Her fingers dug into the soft skin of her own forearms.

She looked quickly away—and her eyes found Snuggles. The dog's eyes were following Brand with a look of blatant hero-worship. She felt somewhat betrayed, and frowned a telepathic message at the animal. We're trying to get rid of this man, Snuggles. He probably would have felt guilty staying more than a week if you had stayed in the chest.

'What have you done to my dog?' she asked, trying to disguise the betrayed pout in her voice.

He shrugged. 'Don't know for sure. Dogs always like me. Dogs and kids.'

'Particularly if you're holding a chocolate bar?' she asked sarcastically, noticing the tell-tale smear of brown on Snuggles's chin.

He grinned—without a trace of sheepishness—

and her heart quickened under the warmth of that look. She lowered her eyes hastily from his. But inadvertently she found her gaze attached to the strong, hard length of his legs. Even while relaxed, his muscles seemed to surge with that leashed power that could explode into such incredible speed and manoeuvrability on the football field.

He turned slightly, and her eyes caught on the long, jagged scar that ran from the side of his kneecap up his thigh, and then disppeared under the border of his shorts. The scar, purple and ridged, brought her no sense of horror. Instead her longing to touch him increased, only this time the longing was different. It wasn't a purely physical reaction, nor was it curiosity or sympathy. No, it seemed to be motivated by the most baffling tenderness, as if her fingertips tracing the edges of that ragged scar could soothe and heal——

'I'm going back to bed,' she announced tightly. She was totally unsettled by the feelings leaping within her because she found herself in the presence of a man with barely any clothes on. She shook her head sadly. There was no doubt about it, she was deteriorating into a drooling old maid! She turned away.

'Shannie——' a strong hand was resting firmly on her shoulder, turning her gently around. '——have breakfast with me. I may be a bachelor, but I've never quite gotten accustomed to eating alone.'

'I bet you don't have to worry about having breakfast alone very often,' she shot back, shaking away from the hand that rested on her shoulder and trying to ignore the tingling warmth that remained, even when his hand was gone.

'I'll put your general cattiness down to the hour,' he said affably. 'Let's eat—you won't feel like such a grouch after.'

'I am not a grouch!' she sputtered. 'And I am not in the least hungry!' The smells of bacon, scrambled eggs and pancakes wafted all around her, so the effort of her last statement was huge.

'Tut-tut! What a way to start the day. Not one, but two lies.' He shook two fingers at her in playful accusation.

'You're an absolute horror,' she informed him, surrendering with good grace, and making her way towards the breakfast nook.

It was incongruous, really—two near-strangers sitting in the intimate little cove of the nook, neither with much on in the way of clothing. An observer coming in on the cosy scene would most certainly have assumed they were lovers. There was an ease between them that was startling to Shannie.

She was also startled that she was enjoying herself so immensely. She didn't feel shy or self-conscious. She didn't even feel her usual early-morning fogginess. She felt alert, wonderfully vibrant, oddly content and completely comfortable sharing this intimate little ritual with Brand.

Maybe, she decided happily, running an inn wasn't going to be so bad, after all. Maybe her mother was right—she'd allowed herself to become too isolated, allowed herself to rate the joys of solitude just a little too high.

'I'll flip you for the dishes,' he offered.

'No, fair's fair. You cooked so I'll do the dishes. It's not too tough with the dishwasher, anyway.'

'I was hoping you'd say that.' He folded his hands behind his neck, and for the first time she was uncomfortable, feeling his dark eyes following her as she moved around the kitchen in her skimpy T-shirt.

'Do you have a boyfriend?'

At the abruptness of the question she turned and looked at him nervously. Would he take the answer 'no' as permission to begin hot pursuit? Was he looking to liven up his days at an old and isolated country inn with a brief fling, that would be quickly relegated to memory once he was on his way? Had she encouraged him by eating breakfast with him in a scanty T-shirt? Could laughing and talking with animation, in a state of some undress, be interpreted as flirting? As more than flirting?

'No,' she said stiffly, her expression uninviting.

'In between?' he asked, but she was suspicious of his interest, not lulled by his casual sip of coffee.

'There hasn't been a man in my life for a long time. Years. That's the way I like it.'

'Why?' His expression of genuine astonishment made her feel as attractive—as entirely woman—as she had ever felt. For some reason the fact that he could make her feel that way—that he could exercise a strange power over her when she didn't want him to—made her furious. Was she that gullible? Had she been born yesterday? Was a wink, a grin and an insincere 'you're beautiful' all he would need to do in order to waltz her right upstairs——?

'Quite frankly,' she told him acidly, 'I have yet to meet a member of your sex who doesn't bore me to death.'

He was up out of his seat in an instant, stalking her across the kitchen floor on stealthy cat's feet.

'A remark like that could be interpreted as a challenge——'

She wished she could read his eyes, but they had gone flat and coldly unreadable. 'Don't be ridiculous,' she stammered, backing away from him. 'I just meant——'

'A remark like that could make a man want to find out for himself what you meant.'

'Could it?' she whispered weakly, still backing away. Her back bumped up against the door, and she nervously began to feel around behind her for the handle, her eyes all the time held in the spell of his.

He caught her hands, and held them to her sides, then slipped his steel-strong arms around her, locking her into helpless immobility. There was no roughness in the gesture—only solid, implacable strength.

Struggle, she ordered herself, but the voice seemed to be coming from a great distance, muffled by the crashing of her heart, the rasp of her breath, the low, hungry cry of something within her so long suppressed that she was surprised it still resided in her at all.

The magnetic power of his eyes seemed to fade slightly, but only because now other sensations began to clamour within her—fighting for their share of her awareness. The sensation of her breasts brushing up against him—separated from the naked wall of his chest by only the thinnest film of cotton—melted the stiffness in her, and coaxed her reluctant surrender. And though that surrender was little more than a silent sigh, he seemed to feel it, to have been waiting for it.

The brown eyes that had been scanning her face suddenly seemed to change colour, darkening to a shade of pitch, smouldering with fires, the intensity untempered by his look of—what? Could it be wonder? Could it be welcome?

His mouth came down over hers, she unaware that she had met him half-way, had been reaching for him with an eager hunger and a curiosity that were inappropriate in one her age.

At twenty-six years old, and in the twentieth century, Shannie Smith was an albatross. She had never been involved in an intimate relationship, she had never indulged in casual sex. In honest fact, she had barely been kissed.

It wasn't that she wasn't interested in sex. Her desires were normal and healthy—she just exercised higher principles than most of her generation thought necessary. And she had been telling Brand the absolute truth. Most members of his sex bored her beyond belief. She had had too much exposure to the athlete friends of her brothers—men she sometimes found physically attractive, but invariably also found unbearably self-centred and intellectually incompatible with her. And she had been exposed too often to men whose interest in her doubled when they discovered she belonged to the famous 'fighting Smiths', as her father and her brothers were known.

The rather grim irony was that, in growing up in a home that always swarmed with athletes, she had come to think of those lean and well developed bodies as normal, when in fact they were a rarity—especially as she grew older. And she was helpless to change the fact that she could not feel so much as a flutter for a man who was her intellectual equal, but who had soft hands and a flabby mid-section.

Added to that, she did not seem to have her girlfriends' remarkable ability to romanticise outrageously; that is, to fall in love frequently simply by reading qualities into people that in actual fact—and in the harsh light of day—did not exist. And she was, at an instinctive level—not in a contrived or prissy way—simply unable to compromise. She was unable, even in her most desperate moments, to imagine sharing an intimacy with just a body—someone with whom she felt no emotional or intellectual bond. She was equally unable to imagine indulging in that most private of acts with someone who did not spark some deep and strong physical yearning within her.

And so, without even knowing it, she was responding to Brand Heaton with a lifetime of pent-up passion, with the glorious joy of a woman who was experiencing something that she had thought she might never experience—that she had almost come to believe was a myth. Without so much as a thought, her carefully maintained principles fell away from her—but in fact, they fell away from her as naturally and with as much ease as she had adhered to them.

She lived so largely in a world of her mind, a world in which the perimeters, the realities, were shaped entirely by her thoughts. Being kissed by Brand was like stepping into an exhilarating abyss—for there was nothing familiar here—words and thoughts existed no longer. The future and the past ceased to be. Suddenly she danced in a world that consisted completely of the moment—that was composed entirely of sensation.

Sensation—soft fire licking through her veins, cool spring water tingling up her spine, an exquisite ache ebbing and flowing in the pit of her stomach, a golden haze of sun-bright yellow filling her, growing more and more intense as she soared higher and higher, instinctively seeking a release that she knew must exist, but that she did not know . . .

Gently, he withdrew his lips from hers, but still he held her close, his breath stirring in her hair like a sigh. Slowly she made the transition from that exquisite universe of sensation, thought seeping slowly back into her mind. And yet it was thought as tinged with gold as the sensation had been. Or maybe it wasn't anything as articulate as thought—just feeling. A feeling of being close to someone, closer than she had ever been. A feeling of being cherished, a feeling of rightness, of belonging. She cuddled deeper into that feeling, wrapping her arms around his waist, nestling her head into the silken pillow of silver-tipped hair on his chest, listening to the steady beat of his heart.

He laughed huskily, a faint tremor in the sound. 'Well, were you bored?'

The comforting dreamy haze that she was wrapped in disappeared with the abruptness of a popped balloon. She yanked herself out of the circle of his arms and studied him with wide-eyed dismay. Good God, what if for him this was nothing more than a masculine game—a challenge he couldn't resist solving, a point he couldn't resist proving?

He pulled her back against him, a hand on her back, trying to soothe away the fear that had flashed in her eyes. 'It makes everything different, Shannie,' he murmured, but she heard his regret and sensed that he was talking to himself as much as her.

'What do you mean?'

'Oh, hell!' He did release her then, looking at her long and hard with troubled eyes. 'It means you're not just a friend's kid sister any more. It means you're not just my landlady.' He looked over her shoulder, thrust his hands into the pockets of his shorts. 'It just makes everything different.'

Now, of course, would be the ideal time to tell him that yes, it did make everything different, and all things considered wouldn't it be wise if he repacked his six suitcases and left? And yet, for the life of her, she could not say that: the words stuck somewhere deep inside her, refusing to allow her to force them out.

'It changes nothing,' she said, steadily. She hoped her voice carried the sophistication of a cosmopolitan woman quite accustomed to passionate kisses, and quite unmoved by them at an emotional level. 'The house is large, and you needn't worry that I'll be expecting to be swept up into your big, strong arms every time we pass in the hall. As long as we both realise it was a mistake——'

'If I thought it was a mistake,' he told her quietly, 'I wouldn't be so damned concerned.'

What was he saying? she wondered dizzily. He couldn't possibly have been as exhilarated, as swept away, as wonderfully overwhelmed as she had been. It had changed her whole world, shaken it on its axis. It would be so incredibly naïve to believe that this feeling was the same for him, the same kind of 'difference' that he was talking about. He had probably kissed a hundred—ha, a thousand—women just like that. How dared he try to pull an old smoothie act on her? How dared he insinuate something special had happened for him? Why, he was moving in for the kill, the callous-hearted Casanova!

'Mr Heaton,' she breathed, grey eyes turned to ice, 'I understand that most athletes believe they were blessed with more libido than the normal mortal man, but I am not interested in being a receptacle for your misplaced passions.'

Anger exploded across his face, and for a moment the threat of physical violence sizzled in the air between them. Then the expression faded from his chiselled features and he ran his hand distractedly through his thick, sparkling hair.

'Why would you try to make it ugly, Shannie?' he asked her quietly and wearily.

You don't owe him explanations, she told herself fiercely. Tell him to go! Now! He was so dangerous. But still, even in her desperation, her confusion, her torment, that solution seemed too final, too severe. He looked sincere. Genuinely hurt. But she suspected she was guilty of still nursing schoolgirl dreams: that this man, so universally adored, was somehow going to fall for her. It was about as realistic as a teenage girl mooning over the glossy photo of her Hollywood idol and thinking, 'if he could just meet me . . .'

She recognised she was every bit as dangerous to herself as he was, because for once pragmatic Shannie Smith might be capable of reading into someone things that just weren't there, of indulging in all too one-sided romantic fantasy.

'Brand,' she said weakly, 'it just happened so fast. Too much, too soon, you know? We're strangers.'

He touched her cheek gently. 'It was just a kiss, Shannie. Nothing to be scared of.'

But if she had reacted that way to one kiss, it was too frightening to contemplate how she would feel if she allowed things to get to the place that such kisses led to.

'But I know how you feel,' he continued softly. 'It shook me, too. Like I said, it made things different. I don't think I'll be able to look at you without thinking about it—without wanting to kiss you again. But you're absolutely right. We're strangers. I don't need the complications of finding out where that kiss might lead. So we'll just back up. We'll go back to just being an innkeeper and an inn customer.'

The doorbell rang and Shannie jumped at the sound, then instantly hoped he wouldn't relate the out-of-proportion reaction to the raw tension she felt. Then, irrationally, she was annoyed when he didn't even seem to notice.

'That'll be my stuff,' he said, shoving his hands back in his pockets as he strode out of the room, whistling. Whistling!

Wonderful, Shannie thought, gazing after him. He was a rational and mature man. Why did she feel like she wanted to kick his good leg out from underneath him?

She did what she should have done an hour ago. She stomped up the stairs and went back to bed. But the damned noise of what she guessed to be at least four thousand pounds of equipment coming up the stairs kept her from returning to the blessed oblivion of sleep. It was, it was, it was! It was *not* the desperate, gnawing hunger that sat in the pit of her belly and whimpered to be fed . . .

She heard the distinctive sound of Snuggles's fat feet clicking up and down the hardwood stairs. Her previously disturbed dog was apparently so under the spell of their charismatic guest that he had forgotten to be perturbed by the presence of the moving men. Furiously, she pulled the pillow over her head, wondering if she was really only trying to stop hearing, or if smothering herself seemed like as good a solution as any . . .

Shannie told herself firmly that the only reason she was going anywhere near Brand's room was because he had been squirrelled away in there all afternoon, and she had no intention of allowing him to miss the dinner she had been sweating over for most of the day. She was not, she told herself, the least bit curious about the nature of the stuff that had been delivered this morning, or the strange noises that had been emitting from his room ever since.

'Come in!'

She entered cautiously, and then couldn't keep the dismay off her face. Her lovely replica of a turn-of-the-century bedroom had been transformed into a jungle of metal bars and weights. Brand was hovering over some piece of equipment that looked like it had been designed specifically to cause human suffering, with a wrench in his hands.

'Looks like hell, doesn't it?' he commented cheerfully, glancing up at her. Did she just imagine a certain grimness underlying the words?

'I could have rented you the basement,' she agreed sourly. 'It might have been a little more appropriate for a torture chamber.'

'Not a bad choice of phrase,' he said thoughtfully. 'Maybe I could hang a few plastic spider webs around, add a rack, and play taped screams.'

'Are you ever serious?' she demanded, feeling like he was shutting her out—deliberately deceiving her with his blithe words that weren't matched by his expression. Her tone softened. 'Is it really going to hurt you?'

'Shannie,' he addressed her sombrely, 'it's going to hurt like hell, and believe me, I won't be laughing.' He looked almost relieved to let go of the façade of good cheer.

'Then why are you doing this?' she asked him, vaguely aware that the soft pleading in her voice did not mirror the attitude of someone who wanted to remain a distant stranger, who had made a pact to be 'just' the innkeeper.

'I have to.' His eyes moved, unconsciously, to a bronze-framed picture on the bureau, the only personal touch he had added to the room aside from his machinery of pain.

Shannie followed his gaze, and felt her face freeze, her immobile features hiding her instant agony of jealousy and rage. He'd kissed her—and he had a girlfriend!

The swine! The cradle-snatching, odious swine! At first glance, the lovely, large-eyed girl in the picture appeared to be not a day over sixteen. But then Shannie realised that it could well be the thick, dark braids, the impish features, the guileless, open smile that gave that illusion of innocent youth. For at a closer look there was something in those steady, dark eyes that was not young at all, for all that it was intensely beautiful. What was it? Whatever it was, it lent the woman a quality of being ageless—she could have been twenty—or ten years older than that. It was impossible to tell.

Reluctantly she unlocked her gaze from the compelling picture and its mystery. 'Dinner's at seven,' she told Brand crisply.

'Roast beef with all the trimmings? Straight out of a cardboard box?' He rolled his eyes, then added with resignation, 'Well, I'm starving. I hope you cooked me two.'

'You'll have enough to eat.' She shut the door with trembling hands.

On reaching the kitchen, she was direly tempted to take the succulent brown roast and the puffy golden Yorkshire puds out of the oven, fire them into the bin, and replace them with TV dinners. With a little effort she could probably even manage to burn the damn things!

Instead, she set the table in the dining-room for one, her mind working feverishly. So now she understood the 'complication' fully. She entertained, with brief and uncharacteristic naïveté, the possibility that the picture might be of a sister or of a favourite niece. But, no, he had not looked at that picture in a way that could be construed as brotherly. He had looked at it as if his very fate was tied to her, somehow . . .

Shannie sighed heavily. If he had been tempted to have a fling with his landlady at the expense of some brassy, brainless blonde, she might have eventually found it in her heart to forgive him—though she doubted it.

But to betray the young woman in that picture by even looking at another woman, let alone kissing her—let alone insinuating something more might happen, if they let it . . .! No wonder he had been troubled, even if his moment of guilt had been disgustingly brief. How could he look into eyes like those eyes—those strange, all-seeing, sad, wise, kind eyes—and admit an act of faithlessness, no matter how small, no matter how impetuous?

Men! Shannie thought with baffled dismay. Didn't they ever know? Didn't Brand Heaton know he had found something too special to risk on an impulsive kiss? So special that it shone out of a flat, dimensionless photo, so special that strangers probably stopped on the street and looked wistfully after that girl, wanting something that she had shining in her eyes, wanting to capture a bit of that elusive spirit.

She heard him thumping down the stairs, pulled herself from her thoughts, and arranged her features into careful indifference just as he burst into the dining-room. She allowed herself one small, self-pitying wince at the masculine vitality he exuded, despite his leg, despite the trace of pain around his mouth.

'Shannie, I've never smelled such aromas.' He took a deep breath and pronounced, 'Ambrosia! I don't care if you do serve it on a tin plate. I'll know it isn't a TV dinner.' He stopped short, looking at the setting for one.

A brow lifted, and his puzzled eyes touched her face.

'I've already eaten,' she informed him coolly.

'Oh,' he said disbelievingly, those dangerously perceptive eyes searching her face.

She turned away. 'You don't mind getting your own off the stove?'

'I guess not.'

She gave the inn customer her best innkeeper smile. 'Well, enjoy.'

Perfect, she thought, once she was safe behind the closed door of the gable-room. She ripped viciously at a piece of stubborn wallpaper she was trying to strip from the wall.

Yes, I handled that perfectly, she congratulated herself again. Her stomach moaned plaintively. Well, almost perfectly. She had forgotten to fix a plate for herself.

CHAPTER FIVE

'SHANNIE!'

The frustrated bellow shattered a week of silence between them. Shannie had diligently locked herself in the gable-room, working with fierce energy on preparing the walls for paint and wallpaper—Brand had rarely left the confines of his torture chamber. He was conspicuously quiet in the mornings. She left his dinner on the stove, and let him fend for himself at breakfast and lunch.

It was almost as if he wasn't there—but of course, she never quite forgot he was. To her indignant surprise she found she slept better at night just knowing Brand was near. She hadn't really been aware of how often she woke up before, her breath caught in her throat, her ears straining against the silence of the big house.

But it wasn't just that she felt more secure— she just felt the strength of his presence, for all that she avoided him. Felt it, and felt comfortable with it, except for the occasional renegade yearning for more . . . like this morning, when she had piled into him as he was coming out of the shower. He'd been unselfconscious, with a towel tied around his waist—a towel that revealed far less than the running shorts he usually sported,

78

she'd tried to convince herself. And yet, there had been something so magnetically potent about him, with the silver-tipped hair on his head and chest curling wetly, his sleek muscles glowing with a clean and velvety lustre. His aroma, soapy and fresh as a cool spring morning, had been more heady than wine.

With a deep breath, she had pushed by him into the bathroom, snapping the door shut behind her and leaning heavily on it. His effect on her would be far too obvious if she posted a sign that said 'Guests must be completely dressed at all times'. Instead, she made her own shower icy cold, and swore never to be in that particular place at that particular time again.

'Shannie!' he shouted again.

She opened the gable-room door and went to the head of the stairs. 'What?' she called down them, keeping her own tone deliberately normal. Sound carried well through the old house—there was absolutely no need to bellow!

'Get down here!'

She bristled. 'Please?' she suggested.

There was a long silence. 'Please!' he finally gave in impatiently.

He was in the kitchen, his arms folded over his chest. He was glaring at Snuggles, who wasn't being in the least perceptive to his mood. The dog pranced back and forth, stub of tail waving gaily, teeth closed stubbornly over——

Shannie squinted at her happy mutt. Over what?

'I want that back,' Brand said tightly, pointing at the navy blue fabric clenched between Snuggles's teeth.

'What is it?' Shannie asked innocently, though she had a pretty good idea. She choked back the laughter beginning to bubble in her stomach. His genuine embarrassment would certainly startle those members of the Press who insisted on casting him as a playboy.

'Never mind what it is! I've been chasing this foolish excuse for a dog around the house for half an hour. The one time I got my hands on—er—that, he wouldn't let go, anyway.'

'You know, Brand, I have brothers. I have seen jockey shorts before.' She managed—just barely—to remain poker-faced.

'I realise that!' he responded with strained dignity. 'What I didn't know was where this idiot would head after he pulled the lightning raid on my room. He was in and out in a blur of motion I wouldn't have thought was scientifically possible, considering his general lack of aerodynamic design. But what if he'd taken his prize under your bed? What if he left them on the sofa? I really didn't want your opinion of me to go any lower than it already is.'

Firstly she was startled that her opinion mattered to him at all, and secondly she was discomfited that the attitude of cool professionalism she had adopted had not disguised the judgement she had formed as the result of a quick look at a picture. Of course, she had cooled down enough to recognise her judgement as hasty and founded on shaky grounds. How could she reasonably accuse him of a moment of disloyalty when she knew nothing about either the relationship in question or the young woman in the picture?

In fact, remembering the context in which he had looked to that photo, it had occurred to her that that lovely, innocent face had something to do with Brand's somewhat desperate effort to make a come-back in football—his pushing himself to the edge of pain and beyond. For the first time, Shannie allowed herself the luxury of wondering if the woman's haunting expression was real, or if it was just an expression—a bratty movie star could learn to look heartbreakingly sweet, after all!

She sensed with unerring feminine intuition that Brand's rehabilitation effort was tied to that girl in a way that was not entirely healthy. Was he afraid he would lose her if he wasn't a star any more? If he wasn't the football hero that head waiters bowed to and supermarket assistants swooned over? Did he not trust her to love him as he was—and not for what he did? Could he not trust her to separate the man from the celebrity? To put himself through a daily regime of agony he must love that girl very much, somehow see his career as way of wooing and winning her. And yet that kind of loving could easily result in a build up of pressure that might momentarily madden him to seek the lips of another woman—

to enjoy a kiss that just was, that demanded nothing and had no price tags attached to it.

Still, for all Shannie's rationalisation, she could not change the fact he was obviously involved somewhere else, and for her that was enough. There was not even much point in admitting that she liked him enough to wish better for him—to wish he was involved in a relationship based on trust and respect, laughter and shared interests, rather than on the celebrity status he was killing himself to retain. No, better just to admit it was none of her business, and avoid him completely.

Shannie sighed. Even if it might help her avoid him to allow him to keep on thinking she had a low opinion of him, she just couldn't do it. She had a temper, it was true—but it was one thing to hurt a fellow human being in a moment of anger. It was quite another to keep on hurting deliberately. And she didn't care if he was world renowned as the big, tough football player. He still had feelings and *nobody* liked to feel disliked or scorned or looked down upon.

'Brand, I don't have a low opinion of you,' she admitted quietly.

His eyes were frankly disbelieving. 'You have a hell of a way of showing it.'

'What do you mean?' Oh! It had been hard enough to say, and then he had the ill grace to challenge her!

'I guess,' he responded silkily, 'I've gotten the distinct impression you dislike me. You eat alone every night. I eat alone every night. If we happen to pass each other in the hall you scurry the other way like you've just come in contact with a leper——'

'Look,' she sputtered, olive branch forgotten completely, 'just because I don't have the time or the inclination to pander to your every need——'

'That's better,' he remarked easily, and grinned at her, that wonderful, charming lopsided grin that had a million hearts to his credit. 'Now can you help me retrieve my—er—unmentionables from that beast you insist on calling a dog——'

Ah! Back to the nice, safe subject of the dog. 'I think I told you once that Snuggles can be quite ingenious when he sets his mind to it. He led you into the kitchen because there's a bowl of Hershey Kisses on top of the fridge, and he'd be willing to exchange your shorts for several of them.'

'Your dog is holding my shorts ransom?' Brand looked at her with disapproval.

'I told you he could be clever,' she said uncomfortably.

'But how can you let him get away with that? That's no way to train a dog. He'll become a total tyrant. He'll be running the house before you know it.'

'I notice you weren't above bribing him with chocolate when you wanted him to do something!'

'That was different.'

'How?' she demanded.

'It just was,' he retorted, then reached into the bowl on the fridge and withdrew one of the tin-foil wrapped chocolates. 'I suppose I have to unwrap it?'

'No, he likes to do that himself.'

Brand threw her a black look, then bent over and showed Snuggles the chocolate Kiss. 'It's humiliating to be manipulated by a damned dog,' he muttered.

Snuggles looked at the chocolate, sniffed and looked the other way.

'What the hell?' Brand threw Shannie a suspicious look, as if he figured she might be part of a plot to make a fool out of him.

'At least three,' Shannie told him matter-of-factly.

'I took a wrong turn and landed in the nuthouse,' Brand groaned. He turned and grabbed a handful of the chocolates and held them out to Snuggles.

With a look that could only be called regally smug, Snuggles set down Brand's briefs, ambled over, filled his mouth with the offering and, cheeks bulging, departed.

'I thought he unwrapped them?' Brand said, trying not to look concerned.

'He does—in the cedar chest.'

Suddenly Brand started to laugh. It was a rich and robust sound that matched the sunshine spilling across the kitchen floor. It also made him extraordinarily attractive—completely erasing

the shadows of pain that usually lurked in the
tense line around his mouth and faint, dark
shadows beneath his eyes. His mirth brought out
the deep laugh-lines that fanned out from around
those almond-shaped eyes, and made him seem
younger, wonderfully vital and vibrant. His
white teeth flashed in brilliant contrast to the teak
of his skin, and Shannie found herself completely
captivated. She laughed with him, admiring the
fact he could still laugh at himself.

His laughter died, her smile faded, and they
stood looking at each other, a faint and familiar
static hiss building in the air between them.

She broke away from the wicked and wonderful promise of magic that she saw in his eyes.
'Well, I should get back to work.'

'I should too, but I need a break. Look, I don't
blame you for avoiding me. I know I'm not the
greatest person to be around right now.' He
paused. 'Come for a walk with me, Shannie.'

She looked away from him, out of the kitchen
window. It was a gorgeous day. A mild sun
splashed down through the trees, dappling the
world green and gold. Birds sang, insects
hummed, cattle lowed in the distance. A magic
kind of lazy, hazy, summer day.

It occurred to her she was missing most of the
charms of summer with her self-imposed exile to
the gable-room, and suddenly nothing could
have kept her from the fresh air—or from his
company. Everyone was entitled to a little magic
every now and then. A little innocent magic,

nothing more. Besides, she wanted to help him 'take a break', forget for a while the torturous expectations he subjected himself to, for whatever reasons he did it.

'Where do you want to walk to?' she asked, as a way of saying yes.

'How about the lake?'

She groaned. 'That's not a walk, Brand. That's a three-day excursion! The lake must be ten miles from here.'

'Approximately a mile and a half.'

'Oh.'

'Look, if a gimp like me can do it——'

'Don't you ever call yourself that again!' she said, her own vehemence taking her by surprise.

'You know, Shannie,' he said tentatively, as if trying out an idea, not just on her, but on himself, 'it's possible I will be, though. Maybe for the rest of my life. Maybe I'm never going to walk quite right again.'

He left something unsaid, but she heard it. 'Especially if you do manage to play another season, Brand? Is that what you're saying? That it could damage your leg permanently?'

His tone suddenly changed, becoming light. 'Ah, nobody knows for sure. Nobody thinks I'll play again, anyway.'

She wanted to ask him why he was doing this, but sensed the futility of it. She had asked before and received no answer. It was obviously an intensely private motivation, an intensely private battle. Instead, she touched his arm.

'You listen to me, Brand Heaton,' she told him, her voice soft steel. 'You couldn't be a gimp if you were in a wheelchair, do you understand? Not if you had no arms and no legs. The people who judged you would be the gimps—not you. Not ever you.'

The electricity was building again, his eyes locked on hers with both question and command. She dropped her hand from his arm, and looked away, suddenly embarrassed. What had brought on such vehemence?

'Let's go,' she requested stiffly.

'Let's take a picnic,' he suggested softly.

Don't push your luck, mate, she said to herself. But it wasn't herself that answered. It was a little demon who seemed to have taken up residence inside her.

'A picnic lunch?' the little devil said. 'That sounds terrific.'

'I'll throw the lunch together, while you—er—go fix yourself up.'

It was then that she realised what a horror she must look—old paint-stained army shirt thrown over a pair of wildly flowered rummage-sale-special trousers. Her hair was hidden under a polka-dotted kerchief, and she knew her face would be streaked with little bits of grime, glue, and sweat. And he had looked at her with desire raging in his eyes a few minutes ago! The man must be sick! Why did she feel so delighted with the attentions of a sick man?

Eagerly she went and changed, unconsciously

choosing clothes that matched a mood growing as buoyant as a bright, hydrogen-filled balloon. She put on red pleated belted shorts, and a white form-hugging tank-top, that she then casually knotted a red striped shirt over. She ran a brush through her hair, applied the faintest hint of make-up—when was the last time she'd worn make-up?—shoved her feet into a pair of red flip-flops and dashed down the stairs.

He was packing the last of the sandwiches into a nylon knapsack. He grinned at Shannie. 'The answer to every man's dreams,' he teased her, ' a woman who can get ready to go out in less than ten minutes.'

Unfortunately, his casual remark only reminded her how much he knew about women. She tried not to sound huffy. 'It's only a picnic. That hardly rates an hour in the bathroom.'

'Well, you could certainly teach Greta Mason a thing or two,' Brand muttered.

Greta Mason? Shannie swallowed. 'The actress?' she asked, with what she hoped passed itself off as polite interest and nothing more.

'Yeah. She invited herself along on one of my fishing trips once. She kept me waiting four hours in her living-room, then made a grand entrance—silk safari suit, make-up three inches thick all over her face, her hair encased behind a shield of sprayed plastic, and her perfume so strong it was wilting her plants.'

He knew Greta Mason well enough that she felt comfortable inviting herself along on fishing trips with him? The voluptuous blonde beauty was becoming a household name now that she starred in a television sit-com about a woman who ran a pet shop that catered to the sometimes bizarre tastes of the very rich. Shannie had seen the programme once at her mother's house—it had served to remind her why she didn't own a television set.

'Did she catch any fish?' Shannie asked, when the real question on the tip of her tongue was, 'exactly where does *this* woman fit into your life?'

'She didn't come.' He grinned with wicked, and fond memory. 'I told her the smell of perfume attracts bears, and while she ran screaming back up the stairs I slipped out the side door and headed for the hills.'

'Are you and Miss Mason quite good friends?' Shannie asked with studied casualness.

He shrugged, losing interest in the subject. 'I don't know if friend is the word for it.'

Well, that could mean any number of things, ranging from his total indifference to the blonde starlet, to the fact that they were lovers. At least it reminded Shannie of the league he played in.

He hoisted the knapsack on to his back with easy strength and held open the door for her. She didn't bother to lock the door, and they set out down the narrow, shady lane that ran by her place, until Brand turned off on a narrow, twisting path through the trees.

It was a pleasant walk—much shorter than she would have imagined. Brand had obviously been

this way many times in the past week. They
followed one behind the other, not speaking
much but enjoying the sights and sounds of the
sunshine-dappled woods. Slowly, Greta Mason,
and 'the angel'—as she'd dubbed the young
woman in the picture—faded from Shannie's
mind.

'What kind of tree is this?' Brand asked.
They'd stopped for a breather in a small clearing,
dominated by a huge gnarled tree, its profusion of
leaves making a bright green canopy over the
entire hollow.

Shannie looked at it thoughtfully, walked
around it once, ran her hands over the trunk with
her brow furrowed. She nodded to herself, and
looked at Brand. 'It's a green one,' she pronounced solemnly.

His deep laughter rumbled through the clearing, once again chasing the preoccupied and
troubled shadows from his face, and once again
having the strangest effect on Shannie's heart.

'Good answer,' he told her, his eyes twinkling
appreciatively. 'I don't know the names of trees,
either—it doesn't mean I enjoy them any less.'
They spent the rest of the walk to the beach
convulsed in laughter as they took turns anoint-
ing the trees with any name that struck their
fancies or tickled their funny bones.

By the time they arrived at the lake, Shannie
felt much the same way as she had that first
morning when they had shared his breakfast. She
felt warmed by his companionship—as comfort-

able with him as she had ever felt with another human being.

At the water's edge he took her hand, and it fitted so comfortably into the warm, hard hollow of his that it never occurred to her to protest. She quite willingly kicked off her flip-flops, and waded with him, leaning more and more heavily against his solid frame—though only because the lake bottom was rocky and uneven. Certainly it had nothing to do with the heat that radiated from him, the delightful electrical pulses that surged through her whenever his hand tightened at her waist, or his legs or torso or chest made contact with her.

Suddenly she found herself enveloped in a swift and rather annoyingly sexless bear hug—his way of expressing the contentment he felt, she supposed, because he turned away almost immediately, his arm still around her shoulder, and surveyed the lake, his eyes lit with appreciation.

'You know, I've had it all,' he finally said quietly. 'I've had all the glitter—champagne and caviare and a penthouse with a pool and my own view of the skyscrapers. I've seen most of Europe. I've made more money than I can ever spend. I've driven the best of cars, played polo with princes, been invited to all the galas, brushed lifestyles with the stars.' He sighed. 'And I've never been happier than I am right now—walking barefoot along a beach with you.'

Her heart tightened in her throat, and had he turned those deep brown eyes to her she might have been tempted to take it personally. But his gaze remained fastened on some far away mountain peak. It was probably the scenery, she concluded—the atmosphere around the Shuswap was magnificent and inspiring. To a man whose life had become cluttered by his own fame, the appeal of its wild simplicity, its isolated tranquillity would be great—for a while. But not for ever. And the girl at his side—well, she would only be included because at this moment she was as much a part of the scenery as the wild green hills, and the silent sapphire water lapping gently at their feet.

'I'm starved,' Shannie announced abruptly, sliding out from under the weight of his muscled arm and feeling an almost immediate sense of loss—a sense of the world turning from colour to black and white, of the magnificent becoming everyday. Obviously she was alone in this feeling.

'Shannie,' he teased, 'the way you eat you should be as big as a house!'

He followed her from the water, and busied himself digging through his knapsack. He spread out a blanket, and then unpacked an enormous amount of food: thick peanut butter and banana sandwiches, apples, carrot sticks, juice, and Hershey Kisses.

'Snuggles's Kisses?' Shannie asked of the latter, raising an eyebrow.

He grinned. 'Imagine that—revenging oneself on a dog!'

They fell into a companionable silence, and ate

facing the water. They had the world to themselves, save for the occasional fishing boat or
sailboat out on the water.

After lunch, Brand lay back on the blanket and,
after only a moment's hesitation, Shannie gave in
to the temptation to do the same. The warm sun
and her full tummy made resisting impossible.

He pointed lazily at a woolly cumulus cloud
drifting over the lake. 'Do you see the dragon?
It's a friendly one, like Puff.'

'Don't be absurd. It's an elephant.'

'Well, not any more it's not. I think it's turning
into a car—yes, definitely a Camero.'

'Volkswagen,' Shannie said firmly.

Neither really noticed that their observations
were coming further apart, that their voices were
growing huskier.

'Castle,' she murmured.

'Uh-uh. Computer.'

Heads pillowed on the arms folded behind
them, two pairs of eyes shut almost simul-
taneously, then two childlike sighs of contentment whispered across the afternoon, and two
people slept, peace evident in their untroubled
faces.

Shannie awoke first, her eyes drifting open.
She regarded Brand with sleepy surprise.

Sometime during the afternoon they had both
slipped out of their hands-behind-head pos-
itions—she was now curled up on her side facing
him, and he was on his side facing her, one hand

resting heavily—almost protectively—across her midriff.

Her intellectual reaction was to squirm out from under the weight of that hand, sit up and move away from him. And yet her emotional reaction ruled her—*it* was quite content to lie here beside him, savouring the physical contact while it was available. Her emotional reaction was just to watch him—to drink in the strong line of his face with a certain greedy appreciation she could never allow to show if he were awake.

And so she watched him, became absorbed in the steady rise and fall of his perfectly sculpted chest, drank in the faint shadow cast by his thick, black lashes fanning along his cheek, and the slight masculine darkening at his chin and in the hollows of his cheeks. She watched the light breeze dance playfully through that spectacular silver-tipped hair, and allowed herself envy, wishing it were her fingers that were free to gently ruffle his hair. She noted every detail of him as if she could never get enough. She even wished, remotely, that she had a camera, or that she was a painter, because she knew this moment would have to end. But if she had a picture of him she could lose herself in it again and again.

She smiled a self-mocking smile. Well, perhaps where Brand Heaton was concerned she was just destined to act like an infatuated teenager instead of the mature and successful woman she was. Maybe indulging in a harmless crush was a stage in life she had missed, and now she had to go back and experience it ...

She was aware, suddenly, that he had joined her in the land of the living. His dark eyes rested on her face, a faint smile, a faint mystery in them.

'Shannie,' he said, his voice gravelled from sleep, a thread of wonder running through it, 'I have such fun when I'm with you.' He closed his eyes. 'You know, my parents were immigrants. The whole concept of fun was kind of foreign in our house. I grew up yearning for this thing that I thought was a part of the American dream, but that always seemed to elude me. When I first turned pro and had all this money, you should have seen me. I pursued "fun" with a vengeance. I went to Disneyland, Vegas, Hawaii, ski resorts, Club Med. I never really found what I was looking for. It was all too contrived. Do you understand?'

'Not really,' she admitted.

'It's like all these places and things are trying to sell you something that's not for sale. Nothing "out there" can give you joy. You've got to feel it inside. Shannie, when I'm with you, I feel it inside, and it makes a nap on a sunny afternoon more fun than the log ride at Disneyland.'

She looked away from him, her eyes shining with tears. And then she knew—or acknowledged what she had known all along. She didn't have a mild teenage crush on Brand Heaton. She loved him. She had always loved him—loved him with a strange inner confidence, an inner knowing, that had made it easy to wait ten years—that had made it the most natural thing in the world.

What a heartbreak this is going to be, she thought cynically, trying hard to drag tomorrow's realities into today, trying to protect herself from the cruelty of the cut that had to come. Her attempt to face harsh realities failed, maybe because her effort to make it succeed was so half-hearted.

Wasn't it enough that today, in this moment, she was more fun for him than the log ride at Disneyland? She planted an impulsive, playful kiss on the tip of his nose, then dashed towards the water. Tomorrow seemed such a blessedly long way away.

CHAPTER SIX

SHANNIE and Brand lingered on the beach until
the shadows lengthened across the water in late
afternoon. Even then they packed reluctantly, as
if sensing that this stretch of rocky sand, isolated
as it was from the rest of the world, was a magic
place for them. Here, he was not Brand Heaton,
superstar, she was not the innkeeper or the
magazine publisher. Their roles had been left
behind them, leaving only two people eager to
just enjoy each other and a carefree day in the sun.
The relaxed setting made that so easy—far easier
than it might have been had they been on a date.
They had been spared the awkwardness of being
two virtual strangers staring across a candlelit
table making stilted small talk.

'We'll do it again,' he promised, resting his
hands lightly on her shoulders as she took a last
wistful look over the lake.

She would have liked to press him. When?
Soon? Tomorrow? Next week? But the questions
remained bottled up within her. They revealed
too much of the secret that glowed warm and
precious within her.

He had been an affectionate and interesting
companion all afternoon, and yet her feelings
must remain a secret still. Affection was not love.

He would probably be stunned—even frightened—if he knew what she was feeling and how intensely she was feeling it. No, better to wait, to see what would unfold with these long days of summer.

The phone was ringing as they came up the path, and Shannie ran up the last few steps and across the kitchen.

'Hello,' she answered with breathless cheeriness.

The voice at the other end did not respond with cheer. The woman sounded strained and tired. She asked to speak to Brand.

Quietly, Shannie handed him the receiver, then busied herself at the kitchen sink, wishing she could summon up the integrity not to listen, listening all the same, and feeling a vague resentment about this intrusion into their world for two.

'Oh no,' she heard Brand say into the receiver, his voice soft and threatening to crack. She glanced over her shoulder. His back was turned to her, but his head was down, his shoulders slumped. 'Should I come? ... OK ... tell Kel I love her ...'

Shannie stiffened. Kel? Was that 'the angel'? A favoured niece? Yet *another* woman, aside from 'the angel' and Greta? His soft voice tugged her back from these tumultuous thoughts.

'I think about her a lot ... yeah, tell her I'm keeping my end of the bargain.' He hung up the receiver and stood motionless, staring unseeingly at the phone.

'Brand,' Shannie touched his arm, fighting back her irrational and immature jealousy. 'What's wrong? Can I help?'

He looked at her, his eyes remote, seeing through her. 'No,' he said tonelessly. 'A friend of mine is sick. Nobody can do anything, un-less——' Something flickered in his ravaged expression, and if anything it was even more terrible to look at. It was the face of a man driven by that most useless of emotions—guilt.

He walked by Shannie as if she wasn't there, and she stood looking after him, baffled. Guilt? In what possible way could Brand be responsible for anyone else's health? Had there been a car accident? But no, with the Press living in his pocket as they did, the whole world would have known if Brand had injured someone in an accident.

But maybe what hurt the most was that, after the closeness they had shared all day, he had without warning shut her out. Closed the door into his life firmly in her face. He didn't want to share what was hurting him, and he certainly did not want comfort. She shivered as she remembered the remote, unseeing expression in his eyes. It was as though she had ceased to exist. She could take it even one step further and say that it was almost as if he was sorry she did exist—that today had existed.

'Oh,' she reprimanded herself grouchily, 'I'm

imagining things.' Was she so selfish and self-centred that she could be jealous of his worry over a friend? Besides, he owed her nothing. Hadn't there been that danger all along? That she would fall head over heels and he would just have befriended a comrade's old-maid sister? It was her fault, she concluded miserably, for moving too fast, for feeling too much, too soon.

Over the next few days her initial icy premonition that she'd somehow lost him as a result of that phone call seemed to be proving true. It wasn't her overly active imagination: Brand *had* changed with the answering of that phone. He was carrying some immense burden on his shoulders, but he was also locked tight into a world no one else was allowed to enter. He worked feverishly in his room, looking at her with an absent lack of recognition when he saw her at all. His face was always pain-contorted, he rarely joined her for meals, or if he did he insulted her by eating hurriedly without looking up from the pages of a journal on sports medicine. He certainly did not suggest a return trip to their beach. But then the affectionate man she had spent that day with was gone as irrevocably as was the day itself.

He ate, worked out, slept, and made a daily phone call—a ritual Shannie avoided being anywhere in the vicinity for since inadvertently overhearing part of the first one. He had been using the hall phone and she had been coming down the stairs.

'Hello, sweetheart,' she had heard, but it was not the words so much as the exquisite tenderness in his voice that had stopped her in her tracks and then sent her tip-toeing back up the stairs, the threat of tears pushing painfully behind her eyelids.

What hurt the most was that all she saw these days was a remote and grim stranger—and yet the tenderness, the sensitivity, and the gentleness that she had always suspected were an integral part of Brand's make-up were indeed there—but only for someone else. Still, she was disgusted with herself for the petty and raging jealousy she felt. What right had she to be jealous? How had he ever encouraged her, aside from telling her casually that he had fun with her? That was hardly a proclamation of undying love!

Still, every time she saw him she felt torn between bitterness and tenderness. Bitterness that he could not be all she wanted him to be— bitterness that he so easily and thoughtlessly shut her out of his life—and yet an aching tenderness, too, to soothe the worry and the hurt from his creased brow, to take the ever-present frown that had settled in his eyes and to give him back laughter and sunshine and dragon-shaped clouds.

She also suspected he was working too hard— straining his leg instead of strengthening it. His limp seemed to be getting worse. His features were grey with pain. Even while he ate he was often absently massaging his bad leg.

It was the strangest emotion of loving anger

that she felt with him—an almost wifely feeling, had she stopped to analyse it. She had to bite her tongue—hard—to keep herself from scolding him, to keep herself from trying to convince him to do things differently, to relax a little, to rest a little. But it wasn't her place, she would remind herself stonily as she turned away from his uneven gait or his pain-haunted features.

'I have to go away for a few days,' he announced one night from behind the pages of his sports magazine. He passed her a cheque. 'Naturally I'll give you the same fee as always.'

She folded the cheque and slid it into her jeans pocket without looking at it. She was painfully aware of the place she occupied in his life. The innkeeper. The landlady. The promise of more had never materialised, and yet she still hated to be reminded of the impersonal business basis for their relationship.

She did feel relieved by his announcement, though. The tension of having him around, of tearing herself apart over him was beginning to tell. She wished she had the guts to tell him never to come back, but that she could not do. Even pain offered her some small part of him that was better than the emotional void he would leave when he was gone for good.

And somehow she hoped that when he came back something would be resolved—that he would be the same as he had been that first morning, and that afternoon they had spent on the beach. Or that she—given a vacation from the overwhelming strength of his presence under her roof—would come to her senses and see what a silly, frivolous child she was being, and manage to talk herself right back out of loving him.

In fact, for all that she *told* herself otherwise, while he was away she missed him dreadfully—to the point where she was forced to admit to herself that she would rather have him here grumpy and indifferent than not have him here at all.

He was gone three days. When he came back, he looked worse than ever—his eyes clouded with pain, his mouth twisted into a grim line.

He glanced at her when he came in the door, oblivious to the fact that she had greeted him with an almost trembling eagerness that all her resolve had still made it impossible to hide.

'Could you see that I'm not disturbed for the next few days?'

She stared at him. What was she, the bloody hotel clerk? What was she, the doormat? Oh please, Mr Heaton, wipe your shoes with my heart? What exactly did he mean? Hold his calls? Keep the stereo low? Keep Snuggles from scratching pathetically at his door? Or did it mean, Keep out of my way, Shannie Smith, Proprietor?

'Yes, sir,' she responded with cold sarcasm.

For a moment he looked jolted, and then he just shook his head wearily, as if her sarcasm was one more thing that weighed too heavily on him. She glared at him. How dared he make *her* feel guilty?

The temptation was great to make sure he was disrupted as much as possible, but somehow she knew she wouldn't. In some small way he had asked her to help him, and she would. She might have even cancelled the Friends of History meeting—had she remembered it.

Instead, on Wednesday afternoon the door chime resounded and echoed throughout the house. Shannie, who had been gardening in the back, raced around the front. Mrs Pikle and Ms Dempster stood on her porch in their summer print dresses, giving her fluttering little waves and calling chirpy greetings.

'Oh, no,' Shannie murmured. Within fifteen minutes, ten more women arrived, and Mrs Casey brought her grandchildren.

'Just throw them in the back-yard, dear. They'll be good.'

Shannie threw them in the back-yard, along with Snuggles, who had been greeting their guests with slobbering enthusiasm that led to more than one shrill little cry over shredded nylons. Soon the kids were shouting merrily, the dog was barking, the ladies were singing their opening song, and the kettle was shrieking. Shannie stood in the kitchen listening for sounds of life from Brand's room. Nothing. Not a sound.

Shocked silence, she guessed, and then shrugged. Well, she had done her best to give him peace and quiet, and she was getting a little tired of tip-toeing around, anyway. Though she rarely joined the meetings, she enjoyed her fortnightly visitors and especially the twittering sound of girlish giggles that erupted from her living-room whenever the Friends of History Society met.

Suddenly a strong arm wrapped around her waist and a husky voice growled in her ear.

'You seem to have acquired a gaggle of geese, Shannie. God, what a racket!' He turned from her and helped himself to a handful of the dainty sandwiches, oblivious to the fact he had destroyed the artistic merit of Mrs Henry-Whiton's carefully arranged plate.

'The Friends of History Society meet here every second week.'

'Couldn't you have warned me? I might have planned a nice quiet afternoon at a rock concert. Besides, what if somebody recognises me? Hell, Shannie, it would be out to the Press in about——'

It was the first time in her experience with him that he was reacting just like the conceited celebrity-athlete he was, and she was rocked by it. She had thought she was in love with this selfish, overbearing, conceited, full-of-himself excuse for a human being? She had been tip-toeing around the house pandering to his eccentric, self-pitying moods—in the name of love? Ha! It was an exercise in defeatism to love someone who didn't love you back—and Brand Heaton, just like every other goddamned superstar was already so in love with himself that there wasn't room for anybody else in his life.

'Look here, big shot,' she hissed, her eyes

spitting icy sparks, 'no one here is going to recognise your big, boring self. Believe it or not, there are people in this world untouched by football—with only the vaguest awareness that it even exists. Those are the only kind of people who are ever invited to my house—and the one time I made an exception, I lived to regret it.'

'Shannie——' He took a step towards her. The remoteness left his eyes momentarily, and was replaced by a dismayed look of regret.

But she had been charmed once too often. 'Just get lost,' she commanded abruptly, turning away from him.

'Mr Heaton? Oh, goodness, it is you!'

Shannie froze, then turned incredulous eyes to Mrs Braton, who had just come in the door and was staring at Brand with the worshipful eyes of a fan.

Brand gave Shannie an I-told-you-so look, and for a moment Shannie feared he would snub his eager little fan, just as he was capable of snubbing the Press. She would hate him if he hurt sweet old Mrs Braton. In fact, it struck her with some surprise that she was half-way on her way to hating him now!

But he redeemed himself slightly by turning to Mrs Braton with a disarming smile.

'Do you remember me?' the old woman asked breathlessly.

Brand looked at her carefully. 'I'm sorry, ma'am,' he apologised gently. 'I meet so many——'

'It was in '81,' she rushed on. 'The semi-final game between you and the Raiders. My husband and I flew down for it. His cousin, Burt, was the stadium manager, and we met you after the game. You signed my autograph book,' she reminded him hopefully.

To his credit, Brand looked genuinely distressed that he couldn't remember her when it obviously would have meant the world to her.

'Oh, well,' Mrs Braton said cheerfully. 'It doesn't matter.' She scrutinised him carefully. 'How's the leg?'

'I'm working on it. I hope to be back in by the fall—but that's a secret.'

Shannie gasped and stared at him. How could he say that? He couldn't mean it? He couldn't! Good God, the man wasn't even walking that well. The only way he was going to play football was if they pumped him full of pain-killing drugs first. Couldn't the damage to his leg be irreparable if he insisted on playing on it while it was so obviously still injured? How could he run? How could he expose his leg to the brutal punishing stress of a few hours on a footbal field? She wanted to kill him for having such an unrealistic view of his limits. No, not kill him. She wanted to love him. Love him so much that he would be convinced it didn't matter if he ever played football again.

'Your secret's safe with me,' Mrs Braton assured him, the thrust of her sharp chin fair warning to anybody who might try to pry it out of her. 'In fact, I won't tell anybody I saw you here, Mr Heaton. Them boys from the Press are absolute devils, and I wouldn't trust my best friend not to let it slip. By geez, I was fighting mad when they printed that picture of you in the hospital. There are bounds to what people have got a right to know, and that there picture was out of bounds. I wrote the editor of our paper and told him so. And I wrote again, just last week when I found out that picture had been nominated for a news award. Criminal!'

Shannie looked to Brand with surprise. Oh no! she thought. Not that dreadful picture of Brand crying. She could feel a lump of compassion rising in her own throat at the look of helpless fury on his face. He just didn't need that one more thing weighing him down right now. She felt as fiercely protective of him as a mother bear of her cub—despite the fact she'd been close to hating him moments before.

'Well, thank you for your support, ma'am,' Brand said, his voice carefully controlled. 'I appreciate it.'

Suddenly Mrs Braton seemed to remember that they were standing in the kitchen of Shannie's house, and her eyes widened and moved from Shannie to Brand, full of question.

Shannie smiled blandly at her. She'd escaped the influence of her famous football family. She'd be damned if she was going to bring up the connection now to explain Brand's presence in her house. Especially not to a dyed-in-the-wool

football fan! She was liked, accepted and re-
spected in this community for herself. She was
not going to allow that to change. She was not
ever again going to be Len and Ray Smith's little
sister rather than a person in her own right.

'Aren't the ladies waiting for tea?' she asked
softly.

'Oh, I suppose so,' Mrs Braton responded,
disappointment etched into every wrinkle of her
lined face. 'It was so nice to meet you again, Mr
Heaton.'

He gave her that warm smile that made women
want to die for the opportunity to throw
themselves at his size twelve feet.

Mrs Braton left, and Shannie crossed her arms
and went to the window. 'Don't you dare say I
told you so,' she warned.

He came and stood beside her. 'Would I do a
thing like that?'

They watched in silence as the Casey children
roared up and down the yard in hot pursuit of
Snuggles. The Casey boy, a stocky four year old,
was supplementing his efforts to bring down the
dog by throwing rocks at him.

Brand frowned. 'That rotten little brat! Hasn't
anybody taught him respect for animals? Well,
maybe if I go out and turn him over my
knee——'

Shannie put a restraining hand on his arm.
'Watch. Snuggles can handle kids.'

Sure enough, Snuggles suddenly lost patience
with the boy and stopped short. The boy tripped

right over the boulderlike, immobile dog. Snuggles sniffed his fallen victim once, licked his face, and then sat himself comfortably right on top of him.

Brand burst out laughing and his laughter raced down her spine, making her feel warm and good again—as if a beam of summer sunshine had burst through the icy, drab chill of winter.

'Honest to God, Shannie, that dog is growing on me.'

'Oh,' she said stiffly. Hell's bells! She was jealous of an unknown girl in a bronze frame, of Greta Mason, of 'Kel', of mysterious phone calls and now of her own dog! This man could slip by her guard so damned easily.

Brand was once again listening to the women in the living-room. He snorted. 'I don't hear a lot of history being discussed.'

'Actually they accomplish quite a bit—though I've noticed business is definitely last on the list. They seem to relegate it to the final fifteen minutes.'

'Why do they meet here?' he asked a trifle plaintively.

'This is one of the more historically interesting houses in the area,' Shannie told him. 'Word travelled fast when I began refurbishing instead of modernising, and I guess they assumed I would be sympathetic to their cause. They were right.'

'What is the history of this house?' Brand asked, evidently having decided to kill time until the 'gaggle of geese' had departed and he could return to torturing himself in peace.

Shannie hesitated, then her eagerness for the subject overcame her wariness of him. 'Well, the house was built in 1893, so when I say it's historically interesting I'm mostly referring to the architecture, the woodwork, the fixtures, and so on. Nobody famous has ever stayed here, and in fact the house's builder didn't contribute a great deal to the history of this area.

'Jake Stone was a simple farmer—at one time all the land you see around here was his. He was a bachelor until his late thirties, and he lived a life of frugal simplicity. The remains of his one-room log cabin are still on that bluff behind us. And then into his dull and uninteresting life swept Annie Bartholomew, a visitor from England. He met her at a community social function and was completely overwhelmed. The story has it that he was totally bewitched by her after one dance. He asked her that very night to marry him and told her of the house he would build for her as a monument to their love.'

'Oh no,' Brand groaned. 'How can the ending by anything but sad with such an unrealistically romantic beginning?'

Shannie smiled a far away, tender smile. 'Cynic,' she chided him. 'That's what's so special and wonderful. I think it's a big part of the reason I like this house so much. There wasn't a sad ending. In fact, from what I can find out, they were magnificently in love until Jake died at the ripe old age of eighty-eight. Annie followed shortly after, but meanwhile they had raised seven children in this house, and this area is still populated with two surviving children, thirty-three grandchildren, and over a hundred great-grandchildren. I've talked to some of the surviving relatives about Jake and Annie, and they all remember the love. They say love rang and sang through this old house. They remember the living-room furniture being pushed back to allow for dancing at parties, remember sliding down the banisters, huge family dinners, staying here overnight and sneaking out of the upstairs windows.' She sighed dreamily. 'Living history. This house isn't an old dead thing. It's alive, somehow, waiting for the next chapter of its history to be written.'

Brand was looking at her, his eyes solemn, something faintly hard in them.

'Why don't you just admit it, Shannie?'

'Admit what?' she stammered, not understanding the moodiness that darkened his eyes.

'Admit that you never bought this house to turn it into an inn. You never bought it out of some avid interest in history, though that may have developed as part of the disguise.'

'What are you talking about?' Shannie whispered.

'You bought this house because you wanted a piece of its magic. You sensed the love as soon as you walked through that door. Now all you need is someone to play Jake, right, Shannie? You

want to write the next chapter, and you know
somehow this house won't ever feel complete
without half a dozen kids running around and
sliding down the banister. That's what you
bought, isn't it, Shannie? The hope of the kind of
family you never had?'

'That's ridiculous!' she spluttered, her indignation very real. 'Why are you doing this? Why
are you making up stupid fairy tales? Why are
you being so damned cruel?'

'Cruel?' He looked surprised and then
abashed. 'I'm sorry, Shannie. I'm on edge. I
didn't mean to take that out on you.'

'Well, it's not true,' she said furiously. 'None
of it!' But she was blinking back tears. It was
true—and the truth was even harder to accept
because she had never acknowledged it on her
own. No, she had believed each of her clever self-
deceptions—that she was fixing these rooms with
such painstaking patience just for herself and her
own enjoyment. That she liked living on her
own—that her work was all-consuming, that her
family consisted of the children who wrote her
sacks and sacks of loving mail every month.

Oh, but hadn't there always been little ghosts
that played in the shadows of her mind? Little
chubby ghosts with red cheeks and fine hair,
who, yes, chortled with glee as they slid down
that banister?

How had he known the secret dream she
harboured and hid—even from herself? And
why, even if he had seen it, had he felt driven to

mention it? Did he find her living alone with a dog and harbouring those dreams so pathetic that he felt duty-bound to make her face reality?

She regained her dignity with effort, and looked at him coolly. 'What difference could it possibly make to you what I plan for the house? What difference could it possibly make to you if I indulge in a little unrealistic fantasy every now and then?' Her voice was rising and she fought to control it. 'In fact, what difference would it make to you if I was running a bootleg business on the side? This is my life, Mr Brand Heaton, and I never asked you to share it, let alone like it!'

'Agreed,' he said remotely. 'By the way, Shannie, where do you hide the TV set?'

Just like that! He barged into the most private part of her life uninvited, and then, with utter and enraging indifference changed the subject.

'I don't have a TV set,' she told him with grim satisfaction. 'I have always felt that it was the medium of morons!' And she didn't care if she did sound like an old-maid schoolteacher. That's what she was! She owed no apologies for the fact.

Brand glared at her. 'The most important game of the season is on tonight!'

'Good! Go to the bar and watch it! Drink in the adulation of your beer-swilling fans! It might improve your mood!'

Suddenly his hand moved over his brow, in a gesture of pain and weariness. 'I'm sorry,' he said in a low voice. 'I didn't realise I was inflicting my moods on you. I don't know what's gotten into me.'

Damn him! She was just beginning to do a good job of convincing herself that she did hate him, that he was proving too darned difficult to live with, and that it was time for their paths to part.

Now she could see his aching vulnerability again, his hurt, the burden he was carrying. Let me in, or get out, she screamed inwardly, though outwardly she said, 'You could probably rent a TV in Salmon Arm.' And, lest he believe he had sucked her in again, she added icily, 'And remember to rent ear-phones too, or so help me, Brand Heaton, at the first sound of a football game I'll throw the damned thing out the window.'

'I do believe you would,' he said solemnly, then turned and limped away.

CHAPTER SEVEN

SHANNIE hated the sound of a telephone ringing in the middle of the night. It was inevitably a talkative drunk calling the wrong number, or worse, bad news. Groggily she reached for the phone beside her bed, hoping it was the drunk. She glanced at the clock. Five minutes past three.

'Hello?'

'Long distance is calling for Mr Brand Heaton.'

She scowled at the phone. Had his football pals, out on a party, decided to call and discuss plays and glory days with their old buddy? On the other hand, it was hardly up to her to screen his calls, and it might be important.

'May I tell him who's calling?'

'It's Trish O'Rourke.' The voice that replied was throaty, definitely mature, and bubbling with a warm vitality that Shannie couldn't miss. Hmph! The 'angel' in the picture frame, Kel, Greta, and now Trish!

It was a good thing that she had decided she hated Brand Heaton, or she would most definitely be almost sick with childish jealousy at the profusion of women who appeared to play roles in his life. She pulled on a housecoat with jerky,

half-awake anger. Imagine his girlfriends calling
here in the middle of the night! Imagine her
being fool enough to go and rouse him instead of
coldly informing Ms Sexy-voice of the time, and
hanging up. Ah, but that might be construed as
an act of jealousy by Brand—and she couldn't
ever let him guess that she was capable of that
emotion in relation to him.

She pounded on his door, almost falling
against him when he suddenly yanked it open
and stood looking down at her with faintly
impatient question. His hair was sleep-tousled,
and he wore only grey sweat shorts. He slept in
the nude, her wayward mind concluded rapidly,
and a fiery blush began to creep up her neck and
into her cheeks as her mind filed this appallingly
intimate piece of knowledge.

'This better be good—it's the middle of the
night.'

She could, of course, apologise, say she
thought she had heard a noise, and then
backtrack to her room and hang up on the
Marilyn Monroe voice—which is what she had
really wanted to do, anyway!

'Tell that to your girlfriend!' Shannie
snapped. 'There's a phone call for you.' She
turned her back on him and stomped back down
the hall, entered her room and started to slam
the door.

She never heard the satisfying crash, because
her motion was arrested by a firm hand. 'Is this
the only phone up here?' he asked, looking over

her shoulder, and remaining aggravatingly oblivious to the fact she was wrestling futilely to slam the door in his face.

'Yes, but——' She let go of the door and glared at him indignantly as he made his way by her, perched himself comfortably on the edge of *her* bed and picked up the phone.

'You don't mind, do you?' He didn't wait for her answer. 'Hello?... Trish!... The time?... After three ... You forgot the time difference? ... It doesn't matter.' His voice grew soft. 'I can tell by your voice it's good news.'

It doesn't matter! Shannie gave him her nastiest look though he was too preoccupied with his call to appreciate it. Head high, she marched to the other side of the bed, tossed off her housecoat and crawled under the covers. To make it clear to him that he just *might* be disturbing her, she turned on her side with her back to him and pulled the pillow over her head.

The call was brief, which didn't give her any satisfaction. He hung up, and she pretended to be asleep—except that Brand was not getting off the bed. She rolled over, and gave him a black look.

'Sorry, Shannie. I'll leave you in peace in just a minute.' He was massaging his leg. 'I seem to have strained something again. Damn,' he muttered painfully, squeezing the muscles in his upper leg with strength that made her wince.

Her anger dissolved and she studied him with concern. Despite the fact that she could see he

was in pain, she could also see that phone call
had done him the world of good—lifted some
enormous pressure from his broad shoulders.
For the first time in days his brow wasn't
furrowed into a preoccupied scowl.

She considered offering to massage the leg for
him, then dismissed the impulsive thought
instantly. Was she insane? Brand Heaton was a
dangerous enough force to contend with in her
house—never mind in her bed—and never mind
offering to bring a little physical contact into the
situation!

'Just go to sleep, Shannie. I'll be fine in a
minute.'

Obediently she turned over, and clenched her
eyes shut. A useless effort because she just knew
that she would never be able to sleep with that
magnificent male body only an arm's length
away. For a few minutes she lay very still and
tense, but slowly her muscles loosened and
relaxed. There was something just a little bit
calming about that weight on the bed beside her,
something in his closeness that made her feel
peaceful and secure, and just slightly drowsy . . .

She awoke to bright sunshine washing cheerfully through the big french-paned windows of
her room. A chilly morning breeze sighed
through the open window and played with the
white lace curtains. She snuggled deeper into the
warmth of her bed, feeling sleepy contentment,
wrapping her arms more tightly around——

Her eyes jerked open wide, and her mouth fell

open. Carefully she turned her head—and came
face to face with a hair-roughened chest, and
realised that her arms were wrapped wantonly
around a very naked waist.

'Brand Heaton!' she rasped, yanking her arms
away. 'You wake up this instant—you, you
scoundrel! You perverted fiend! You sly——'

Brand murmured in his sleep, rolled over and
sighed contentedly into her hair, wrapping one
arm protectively around her. Her fists clenched
at her sides as she fought the absurd temptation
to just snuggle back into him, and to return to
sleep for a few minutes—or to pretend to sleep
while she savoured his warmth, his scent, his
textured skin.

'Brand Heaton!' she cried shrilly. A small edge
of panic had entered her voice.

His eyes flicked drowsily open, and then
registered pleased surprise. 'Gosh, you're beautiful in the morning,' he said thickly, reaching
up and running a reverent finger over a honey-
coloured strand of her heavy hair.

'What are you doing in my bed?' she muttered
through clenched teeth.

He looked startled, and then frowned in
consternation. 'Oh, hell!' He unwrapped his arm
from her and rolled over on his back, one arm
resting on his brow. 'I was massaging my leg. I
must have fallen asleep.' He looked under the
covers with sudden alarm and then grinned
sheepishly at her. 'It's OK,' he told her. 'I'm
decent. I still have my shorts on.'

'Wonderful,' she said tightly.

Whatever guilt he had managed to feel was already gone, and he was looking around the room with interest, apparently unaware that Shannie was exceedingly uncomfortable—lying stiffly away from him, her thick hand-made quilt pulled primly up around her chin.

'It's wild cherry, isn't it?' he asked with enthusiasm, looking at her chest of drawers then sitting up on one elbow to run a hand along the headboard behind him. 'And the bedposts are hand-carved?'

A bit of her wariness faded, despite the naked, bronzed chest, and the sculpted shoulders now on brazen display. So what if it was a trifle bizarre to be lying in bed beside a man she barely knew, discussing furniture? It was also faintly pleasant.

'It is wild cherry,' she confirmed. 'I got it from a woman who said her great-grandfather carved it in the hill country of West Virginia. He couldn't read or write, he lived in abject poverty trying to eke a living out of a rocky piece of mountainside, and he drank moonshine in copious amounts. Yet when you look at this furniture, none of that matters. What survived was the artisan's soul and the creative spirit that must have been at the core of the man, even if his life-style frustrated it.'

'I can almost picture him,' Brand told her, getting into the spirit of the conversation. 'Big as an oak tree, huge gnarled hands—and yet a faint suggestion of a gentleness under that weathered and wary mountain-man's face.' For a moment they both silently contemplated her furniture, an unknown man, and a different time and world.

Then Brand looked at her, his expression intent. 'You and I feel things the same, Shannie. I've never really experienced that before.'

She flushed, annoyed with herself for feeling sweet-sixteen shy. But it was just like last time. Then she'd been 'fun'. It hadn't gone anywhere and it hadn't meant anything. It was just an offhand comment that he meant nothing by and that she recognised she was all too willing to begin building castles around.

'How is it you knew this wood was cherry?' Her tone was carefully impersonal. 'I'd guess only one in a hundred people would know that. How is it you're one of them?'

'You don't want to hear my life story, Shannie.'

But she did. Considering what an enormously popular public figure he was, as far as she knew nothing had ever leaked out about his early life. She didn't even know where he was from originally. What had he been like as a boy? What adventures and misadventures had shaped him into the mature, strong individual that he was? What kind of background had given him that rare kind of confidence that left him relatively untouched and, she assumed, unchanged by the star status that would have gone straight to a lesser man's head?

'I guess I wouldn't mind hearing your life story,' she said in an I've-got-nothing-better-to-do tone.

'OK, I'll tell you all my secrets—on one condition.'

She was instantly on the defensive. He was going to ask her to keep anything he told her to herself! As if she would go running to the Press! How dare he show so little faith in her! She wanted to brain him—to hit him over the head as hard as she could and then push him out of her bed, haul him over to the window and do her damnedest to drop him out . . . and who wanted to hear his stupid life story, anyway?

'If I tell you mine, you have to tell me yours.'

His request was so different from the scenario that she had just created in her head that her mouth fell open. 'I thought you were going to ask me to sign a pact of silence—in blood,' she admitted wryly.

He looked surprised, then cupped her chin in his hand and searched her eyes. He smiled at her. 'I don't have to tell you that. You don't have the look of a blabber. Besides, once you've heard the story you'll understand, and Shannie, I just know that somehow you couldn't hurt me.'

She felt herself go pale under the warm scrutiny in his eyes. Oh God! Did he know, then? Did he know how much in love with him she really was? Was it so obvious? So obvious that he could look at her, and declare with absolute confidence that he knew she could never hurt him?

Naturally, the wisest thing to do in this moment would be to refrain from stroking Brand Heaton's massive ego by simply telling him that she wasn't the least bit interested in hearing his life story after all, and then kicking him out of her bed, her room, her house, and her life.

Instead she folded her arms over her chest. 'Shoot,' she invited solidly.

'Well, I told you my parents were immigrants, right?'

She nodded. He'd mentioned it that day by the lake—and, like everything else he'd said, it was now engraved on her mind from reliving that afternoon several thousand times.

'They came from Poland right after the Second World War.'

'Heaton's not a very Polish-sounding name.'

'It was changed—like hundreds of immigrants' names were changed—by an impatient immigration official. It was——' He pronounced something totally unintelligible with proud flourish.

'Oh,' she said, inwardly sympathising with the harried official.

'Anyway, my dad was a cabinet-maker. He set up a small business that never did that well, simply because he insisted on putting so much time and quality and heart into every piece. My earliest memories are of him sitting at his workbench, the smells of good wood and varnish thick in the air around him. I used to love hanging around his shop. It was magic for me to see a piece of wood slowly take on life and shape. But most of what I know about woods came through the process of osmosis, because he never encouraged my interest in his trade.'

'Different from most fathers,' Shannie commented. Her own brothers had started throwing miniature footballs when they were still in nappies.

'Maybe just different from most North American fathers. You see, he didn't feel he'd come to the land of oppportunity to raise a cabinet-maker. He could barely read or write, and he was ashamed of his simpleness. He wanted more for his family. He revered education—possibly because circumstances had never allowed an education for him or my mother. A chance for their children to learn, that was why they came to America. They saw that as the only goal worthy of a human being given the freedom to choose it.'

'Oh-oh,' Shannie guessed.

'Right,' Brand said wryly. 'My two sisters quite happily lived out my parents' highest hopes and ambitions for the new world. One is a doctor and the other is a pianist. But me,' he looked at his hands, 'well, I'm no dummy, but I like physical things, working with my hands. I would have been a carpenter, and a damned good one, if my father had offered the slightest encouragement. As it is, to my mother's and father's abject horror, I make my living by the most frivolous and useless of means.'

'Oh, Brand,' she breathed sympathetically.

'Their words, not mine. I'm proud of what I do. I'm good at it. I love it. I entertain millions of people. I've managed to come to terms with the fact that my parents simply don't understand that aspect of America.'

She tried to be tactful. 'If you're so proud of what you do, why is publicity such a bane to you?'

'Maybe because you never do quite exorcise yourself of your parents' beliefs,' he admitted thoughtfully, 'though I honestly think it's more because I'm simply a very private person. I knew from the start that if I ever gave in to pressure from the Press to start revealing little titbits about my private life that I would lose something of myself that I need. When I'm on the field I'm public property. The rest of the time I belong to myself.'

He smiled self-mockingly. 'I guess there's a bit of the old world in me, too, that I can't do anything about. I think we pick the wrong kind of heroes. My father is a better woodworker than I am a football player. Shannie, you would love what he does with wood. It comes alive under his touch. His pieces glow with a vitality and life that's extraordinary. But nobody is ever going to put him on the front page for that. He's never going to be famous. Neither is the plumber who works hard and honestly, perfecting his trade and doing his work with pride. But I'm famous—because I can catch a ball and run fast. It's all out of proportion. And since I don't put much stock in how Americans choose their heroes, I guess I just choose not to be one.'

'You can't make that choice,' Shannie told him gently.

'I can sure as hell try,' he replied with a lop-sided grin. 'At least I don't use my so-called fame to sell cereal to little kids. Now that's enough of that. I want to hear about you— everything.'

He propped a pillow up behind his back for greater comfort, folded his arms over his chest, and looked at her expectantly.

Oh, hell! She hadn't really agreed to play this game, had she? 'There's really not a lot to tell, Brand. It won't interest you, and I want to get up now, so would you kindly get out of my bed?'

'Uh-uh,' he said easily. 'No deal. And I certainly hope this story is going to include an explanation of what Shannie is short for. It's been driving me crazy. Shannon is too obvious, isn't it?' he asked hopefully.

'Far too obvious,' she agreed drily, 'and, no, that little morsel was *not* part of the agreement.'

He gave her a mock-mournful look, then prodded her with his elbow. 'Get on with it, Shannie.'

'Well,' she started awkwardly, 'I was born in Edmonton, and I'm the youngest of three, and the only daughter. Also the only non-athlete. My Dad had a short career as a professional football player before he was injured——' Her eyes clouded, and she seemed to forget Brand was only two inches away. 'He was hurt for the rest of his life—bad back, so debilitating he couldn't work. It's like he went from the hero to the nothing in three excruciating seconds at the bottom of a pile-on. He never really satisfied his thirst for glory. My mother shared that thirst— in fact, both of them seemed to be almost consumed by it. They lived their lives vicariously through their two stocky young sons. I wasn't of any use to them,' she acknowledged in a sad, low voice. 'I don't mean they didn't love me—they just didn't ever seem to know what to do with me. And nothing I did was ever enough to win some of that attention—a look like the one I saw on their faces when Len scored a touchdown or Ray appeared in the paper yet again. I used to write things for Mom, and she'd look at them and then give me this strained, puzzled smile, and say, "Well, isn't that nice, dear?"'

Shannie brushed impatiently at the large tears that splashed down her cheeks. 'I'm being silly,' she chastised herself gruffly. 'Gosh, you'd think I was beaten. It's a good family and I love them. I just never felt I belonged. I wasn't good at the right things—oh, I hate self-pity!'

'Want to trade families?' Brand suggested with gentle humour. 'I mean, I think I would have fitted in just fine with the Smiths, and I think the Heatons would have rather liked a writer in the family.'

Shannie gave him a watery smile, and he seemed to fight with himself and then be unable to resist wrapping his arms around her and pulling her to his chest. A large hand stroked her hair.

'You just go ahead and cry. Get it all out of your system. You've kept it in far too long.'

She sniffled loudly, severely regretting the fact she did not cry anything like a Hollywood heroine—silently and glamorously. No, she rarely cried, but when she did she gave it her whole heart and soul. Her eyes were not hauntingly misty—they were red-rimmed, and probably growing bloodshot. The tears were not trickling down her cheeks one graceful drop at a time, but gushing down in rivers. Her nose was red, and her lips twisted downward in a pathetically childlike expression of woe. She was disgusted with herself and yet she could not stop the embarrassing flow of tears.

'I'm sorry,' she choked, trying to laugh at herself. 'I don't know what's gotten into me. I'm no baby! I never have been, for pete's sake.'

'Shhh,' Brand commanded. 'Maybe you've tried for too long to be tough emotionally because you couldn't be tough physically, like your brothers. Maybe you've tried for too long to hide that sensitive side from people who just couldn't understand it. But you can let it all out now.'

She pressed her wet nose harder into his chest, fearful. 'Will you understand it, Brand?' she whispered, almost hoping he would not hear her.

But he heard her. 'I'll understand, Shannie. Remember? We have something in common. We're both the family black sheep. I had my long, dark night of the soul where I had to come to terms with that.'

'I wonder why I didn't?' she murmured, feeling that heavy, somehow pleasant exhaustion that comes after a good cry.

'Maybe because our society makes it easier for a man to choose his own path—to go his own way. Even expects it of him. But women are kind of brought up to seek more approval. I think it makes it harder for a woman to go against the grain of her family and do what she wants to do. It probably even makes it tough to choose to be yourself.'

'You've got that right,' Shannie agreed, marvelling briefly at his sensitivity. 'My mother seems to think my only chance of redeeming myself, of proving my merit as a "fighting Smith", is not to make it on my own—which I've done, and she seems to ignore—but to marry a football player, preferably a star. I guess that's why I have it in for football players,' she offered, as a bit of an apology for that first night, 'because I've had so many forced on me as if in some way my being an extension of them would

make me more acceptable. To my own family!
Isn't that disgusting?' She sighed. 'Maybe that's
why I avoided relationships altogether. Because
I wanted to be recognised for me, and for what I
could do and accomplish—not for the man I
could catch.' She sighed again. 'But to be
realistic, I could head IBM and my mother still
wouldn't think I'd truly succeeded until I had a
wedding ring on my finger.'

She realised she was babbling, and her eyes
felt weighted. 'Brand, I'm going back to sleep,'
she told him huskily.

'No kidding,' he teased, running a tender
finger over dropping eyelids. 'Shannie, I respect
what you've done with your life. I think it's
terrific.'

'Don't spoil it, Brand,' she admonished him
with sleepy sternness. 'I won't be able to trust
you if you only say things to make me feel good,
and not because you mean them.'

His chuckle was low. 'You're the most
suspicious woman I ever met, Shannie Smith! I
should be downright insulted to be accused of
false flattery.'

'Ha! Brand, you don't even know what I do! I
certainly don't support myself running an inn
with one guest.'

'Ha, yourself. I have a nephew who is *Kids'
Corner's* biggest fan—and probably its most
prolific submitter. I've been known to take his
back issues home with me—though don't let it
get around that Brand Heaton has spent many a

night alone in his penthouse chuckling over a kids' magazine. I have an image to think of.'

'Sometimes I think you're the nicest man, Brand Heaton.' It slipped out. A sleepy admission that didn't seem quite real.

'Sometimes? You're brutally frank when you're nearly asleep, aren't you?'

She nodded unapologetically, and silence fell. She could feel him relaxing too, the rhythm of his breathing slowing to match hers. His heart thudded comfortingly beneath her ear, and his hand still moved slowly and soothingly over her hair. He smelled wonderful—clean and fresh and masculine. Oh, God, she loved having him here—loved it far, far too much.

But who was she kidding? Tomorrow he could well be that remote stranger again. Tomorrow the game, and his other life might have reclaimed him again.

Besides, a long time ago she had sworn she would never marry a professional athlete. Never! But now, with sudden insight, she wondered drowsily if that vow wasn't just a subconscious way of thwarting her mother.

A bell rang inside her head, a light went off. Mother!

'Brand, do you know why you're here?'

'I thought I did,' he said, his voice as drowsy as hers, 'but I have a feeling I'm about to be set straight.'

'My mother,' she informed him.

'Your mother?'

'Matchmaking.'

'Oh.'

A long, long silence, and she was drifting again, floating, too comfortable to even feel indignant with her mother. Too content to throw Brand out right now on the principle of the thing—and then to call her mom and tell her. She was dreaming in fact, and the dream made her smile. She dreamt a deep male voice murmured, 'Well, mothers do sometimes have an instinct for these things.'

CHAPTER EIGHT

WHEN Shannie awoke again, the place in the bed beside her was empty. If there wasn't a tell-tale hollow in the pillow, Shannie would have been very temped to think she had dreamt the whole episode.

Her door had been left open a crack and the sound that drifted through effectively doused her romantic notion that Brand might be downstairs fixing her a breakfast tray—complete with a red rose. Why should he be doing that, anyway? she demanded grouchily of herself. Nothing that could be construed as the least bit romantic had passed between them.

No, Brand was back in the torture chamber—she could hear the distinctive squeak of a weight going up and down on a pulley. She sincerely hoped it fell on his attractive, silver-tipped head!

Damn, if she didn't feel like a yo-yo at the end of his string! One minute he would be holding her in the palm of his hand, the next casting her away, but always, always the invisible string, so that he could call her back.

Not that it was exactly his fault that she was ready to zing back up that string at the slightest indication from him. Well, she certainly wasn't going to sit around here all day waiting to be rewarded for loving him with one of his smiles, or a short conversation, or a pat on the head. No sir, Shannie Smith had some pride left, and she was deserting ship!

She packed a lunch and put a change of clothes and her beach things into her little blue Honda station wagon. She drove to a crowded public beach. The sky was cloudless, the water was warm and inviting, the people around her colourful, lively and interesting, and her book engrossing. But, despite the fact that she tried valiantly to convince herself otherwise, she had a terrible time. Silver-etched on to the back of her mind was a picture she couldn't get rid of—of her and Brand walking hand in hand along a different shoreline, of her and Brand lying side by side in the sand.

She felt something like panic. She had always liked water. She loved being near lakes and water and beaches. That was part of the reason she had moved here. Had he gone and ruined that for her for all time? And what about her house? Could she ever be totally happy there by herself again? Or would a part of her not always listen for the sound of an uneven step on the stair, a tuneless, wonderfully deep voice raised exuberantly under the spray of the morning shower? Would a part of her always turn every corner wishfully hoping to see a broad, muscled back, a silver-tipped head?

She chided herself for being melodramatic. Brand would go, and she'd recover immediately. It would be almost as if he had never disrupted her life at all. After all, if she was going to be realistic, nothing concrete had happened

between them. There had been no mad declar-
ations of love, no promises of for ever. After all,
there had only been one wildly passionate
moment—and by both of their admissions that
had been a mistake.

No, all there had been was a few moments of
laughter, a few moments of easy friendship. All
there had been was a shared interest in old things,
a sense of humour that meshed, a background
that shared a few similar hurts.

All there had been was that wonderful sense of
having become complete after walking alone too
long, that heady sensation of homecoming, of
having discovered something long searched for in
the depths of those clear, brown eyes. All there
was, after all, was those eyes resting on her with
wonder, or with mischief, or with that strange,
glowing light that sent a shiver up her spine, and
made her feel cherished, and alluring, and like a
woman.

No, she told herself firmly, nothing had really
happened between them, and once he was gone
that would be that.

'I'll never get over him,' she admitted out
loud, her eyes misty and unseeing on the water.
'Never!'

Angry with herself for letting that admission
slip out, she ran to the water's edge, dived cleanly
in, and proceeded to swim until her arms ached.
The water running down her face could never be
miscontrued as tears.

After her exhausting swim, she forced herself
to loll in the sun some more, as if she were just

another of those carefree and laid-back, bikini-clad and tanned women who dotted the beach.

Finally, near supper-time, she used the public changing room to pull on a bright yellow sundress and to add a touch of make-up to her sun-kissed face. She wasn't ready to go home yet. She wanted him to be wondering where she was—to maybe even be a little worried about her. She was desperate to believe that he shared her feelings at least that much.

She tried to convince herself that she really wasn't dying to run home and see how he was, see if they couldn't recapture some of the closeness she had felt with him this morning. She *wanted* to believe she was having fun without him—to recapture some of that joy in her own company that she had never been dissatisfied with until now.

She drove into Salmon Arm. 'Everybody knows salmon don't have arms,' Brand had commented once, and she had laughed uproariously, mostly because that was the very same thing she had said when she first heard the town's name—and nobody had thought she was the least bit funny.

She drove around for a while, pretending to be full of purpose. Finally she drove up to Orchard House. It was a beautiful old home that had been turned into a restaurant. She occasionally bought herself dinner there as a special treat—immensely enjoying comparing the restaurant's renovations to her own, looking out on to the overgrown orchard, inspecting the paintings of local artists that hung on the walls. But tonight it crept into her mind that Brand would love Orchard House, and her traditional enjoyment was spoiled. She picked at her exquisite meal, and downed three glasses of white wine rather rapidly.

Brand wouldn't or couldn't come here, anyway, she consoled herself. His precious privacy might be invaded. His profession had given him a profile that forced him to be a recluse. So, what fun would it be never going out—or if you did go out, being swamped by fans wanting autographs? But then what was the use of even thinking about it, anyway? Brand had never asked her out—probably never would. In her wine-induced self-pity, she didn't think about how little she went out, anyway, how utterly content she was to stay home with her dog and her stereo and her books and her house and her magazine.

After dawdling over dinner she forced herself to go to a movie. She sat unseeingly through *The Monster Who Ate Mars* twice, and then went home, her heart pounding in her chest as she got closer. Would he be up, pacing the floors? Or would he be sitting on the sofa pretending to read? Would he offer her a nightcap? Would they talk late into the——?

With a sigh, she realised that she had just defeated the purpose of her whole day. With an even deeper sigh, she pulled into her drive and noticed all the lights were off—her house was as dark and uninviting as if she lived there totally by herself.

She dragged herself up the stairs to her room,

flopped into bed and stared at the ceiling. Did this
mean she had to repeat the whole foolish exercise
tomorrow? How many days would she have to be
gone for before he noticed? Would he ever
notice?

It was a two-fold game, really. One to prove
that she could live and function quite nicely
without him, and two, failing in that, to get him
to acknowledge that he couldn't live and function
without her. Why, she asked bitterly, in a family
of pragmatists, had one noodle-headed dreamer
come along?

The next morning she noted with some relief
that it was as grey and gloomy outside her
window as it was inside her heart. Definitely not a
day for the beach. She could start stencilling the
border of stylised duck decoys that she'd designed
to match the wallpaper in the gable-room.

'Shannie, can I come in?' Brand didn't wait for
an answer, but came bounding in the door in
those sexy navy-blue running shorts, Snuggles
right behind him. They both settled themselves
happily on her bed.

'There's an authentic Finnish sauna not far
from here, Shannie. Did you know that?'

'No,' she said coolly, fastening her eyes on the
window and not his hairy legs.

'Let's go tonight,' he suggested, apparently
not noticing her coolness.

'No,' she repeated firmly.

'Another date?' he asked, with somewhat silky
disinterest.

Another date? Aha! Her mood picked up

immediately. Then he wasn't completely oblivious to the fact that she had not been around yesterday. She regarded him with slightly more kindness, though her answer did not change.

'Look. Shannie,' he looked down at his big, famous hands, and she noticed they were knotting and unknotting uneasily, 'I know I haven't been easy to live with the last little while—damned difficult, in fact. I'm sorry.'

It hit her like a ton of bricks that she trusted this man. She knew that if she could not trust his sincerity now she would never be able to trust her judgement of another human being again as long as she lived. There was not a doubt in her mind that he was deeply troubled, and sincerely sorry about the way he had been behaving. She could feel that familiar sensation of melting, but it was unaccompanied by her usual suspicion that she was being taken in.

'A perfect night for a sauna,' he said persuasively, looking at her face, and pressing his obvious advantage. 'It's really nice when it's rainy and damp. Besides, it helps my leg,' he concluded, mercilessly playing on her sympathetic nature.

'I haven't ever had a sauna,' she admitted slowly.

'Really? It's an experience no one should be without—especially an authentic one like this one. Wood-heated, right beside a creek.'

'Well, it might be fun to try it,' she gave in dubiously.

'I'll book it for tonight, then.'

'Fine.' She watched him go, and sighed. Didn't he know how his look of pure delight at her acceptance led her on? But slowly another thought occurred to her. Maybe, just maybe, Brand Heaton did really care about her. When had her self-confidence taken such a nose-dive that she didn't believe that his interest could be real? She got up and looked at herself in the mirror. Large, solemn grey eyes looked back. Well, she wasn't any Greta Mason, but she wasn't chopped liver, either.

Besides, she'd been told once or twice that she was a fun and interesting companion. Why should she doubt it? Why should she doubt that Brand Heaton could fall in love with her? Her brothers, though admittedly not in his league, had been chased by their share of glamour-pusses. But when it had become time to settle down, they had both just picked ordinary, girl-next-door types of women for their wives.

As for all those 'other' women who littered his life, who was she to judge him? He was certainly allowed to play the field until he found what he was looking for. What did she expect of him? That he would lead a stark and monkish existence until the right one—Shannie Smith—just burst into his life?

She decided it was even acceptable for him to think, however falsely, that he was in love with someone else—until the real thing came along and showed him the difference, of course.

She realised that for the first time she was actually considering the possibility of a future

with him—possibly because with each passing
day it grew more painful to think of a future
without him. She wondered if she was going
crazy—or if she had really seen enough in his eyes
to justify this different way of looking at him—
not as an unattainable dream, but as a flesh and
blood man, who needed just as she needed.

She loved him. Wasn't it worth risking such a
paltry little thing as pride to see if he returned the
feeling? To find out once and for all where she
stood? It would be downright cowardly just to let
him walk away because she was too damned
insecure to believe in herself—to reach out to
him, in love.

Somehow, she thought, tonight would be a
turning-point in this relationship. The very
thought set her heart hammering against her
throat. If it was meant to be, it would simply be,
she told herself sternly. There would be no need
to try and manipulate him or impress him or win
him. It would only be worthwhile if it was real,
anyway—if he loved the real Shannie Smith and
not some mask she had put on.

Still, it would be perfectly all right to do her
best to stack the cards in her favour by making the
most of her assets. She dived for her cupboard.
What exactly did one wear to a sauna?

She wore no cosmetics—she did have a vague idea
that sweating was part of this experience—but
she really didn't need to be made-up. Her skin
had a golden and healthy hue from her day in
exile on the beach, and her eyes had a spectacular

sparkle that no make-up brush, no matter how clever, could have created or improved on. She had once read somewhere that a woman in love produced a natural beauty, a deep and ethereal inner glow, but she had dismissed the theory as so much romantic nonsense. Now she was willing to give it some credence.

She had knotted her heavy mane of hair on top of her head. And then pulled down a few curling wisps to frame her face. The effect was just right. Though practical and casual, on her the hairstyle held a suggestion of sensuality. It exposed the long curve of her neck and subtly emphasised her best features—the large eyes, the sweeping lashes, the soft mouth. Besides, out of some cobwebbed corner of her subconscious she recalled the fact that most men fantasised about being the ones to let down piled-up hair. More romantic nonsense, but what the heck—she was entitled to one foolish romance in her life, wasn't she?

She wore a peach-coloured, oversized shirt with a distinctly masculine cut—the masculine line accentuating everything feminine about her, particularly since she had the shirt belted at her tiny waist. To that she added a pair of white, narrow-legged trousers, and sandals. The whole look was just the right combination of casual and chic—she knew because she had modelled the outfit after one she'd seen while flipping through *Vogue* at the supermarket check-out. In her bag was a large, bright towel, and a daring one-piece pale turquoise bathing-suit.

They drove in silence, and in her heart was a wonderful, bubbling lightness, even though they were now enveloped in slashing rain and a night so dark she couldn't see the road ten feet in front of them.

'Perfect for a sauna,' Brand declared, apparently unperturbed by the weather conditions. He drove with casual skill and confidence, despite near-zero visibilty.

Shannie peered into the night. The landscape had been sucked up by darkness and she could see no landmarks. 'If you can *find* the sauna,' she challenged lightly.

He shot her a grin, and almost immediately turned off the road on to a gravel, tree-lined lane. The road twisted down a hill and around several bends, and then, suddenly illuminated in the darkness, looking golden and inviting in its glade of trees, was a small log cabin with a creek gurgling beside it.

'Oh, Brand,' she whispered as she got out of the van. She could smell woodsmoke in the air, and the tartness of damp leaves. She followed him up several shallow steps and stood in the doorway. It was a simple little place—a few colourful, handwoven Finnish rugs tossed over a cement floor, a table under a window, several wooden benches, and a fire burning cheerily in a brick fireplace. A bottle of wine and two glasses stood on the table.

'No wonder you could find it,' she said wryly.

'OK,' he admitted with a smile, 'I made a trip out earlier. I wanted it to be extra special for you,

Shannie, since it's your first one. The sauna is through that door there—and also a kind of scrub-down room.'

She looked hastily away from the door in question, since right beside it hung a board displaying Finnish postcards of a number of very naked people enjoying their sauna.

'Surely we don't——?' She looked at him pleadingly. It would spoil everything if he expected her to——

His eyes moved to where hers had been. 'Only if you'd feel more comfortable that way,' he teased wickedly.

'I most certainly would not!'

He shrugged, a merry light in his eyes. 'The Finns just have a different approach to their bodies, Shannie. Families and friends sauna together without giving it a thought. Now, why don't you slip into the scrub-room and change, and I'll pour a glass of wine?'

She welcomed the suggestion, since she was already beginning to notice a damp, muggy heat permeating the tiny cabin. In the other room she changed and then lingered, admiring the little hand-made wooden buckets and peeping into the sauna—anything to delay her re-entry into the other room in her bathing-suit. Wryly, she remembered a catchy and ancient little tune about a girl who wore an 'itsy-bitsy, teeny-weeny, yellow polka-dot bikini' and was reluctant to leave the locker-room because of it. But finally, taking a deep breath, she marched back out.

Brand let out a low, admiring whistle.

'Oh, go change,' she ordered gruffly, grabbing a glass of wine and dashing it down in an effort to hide her blush and her discomfort.

'Go easy on that Shannie. It'll hit you hard in here.'

Brand had plugged in his portable stereo while she was gone, and now the warm notes of a classical guitar filled the tiny cabin. She sat down at the table, and sipped her wine—with a little more caution.

Brand rejoined her, totally unselfconscious in white bathing trunks. She had now seen him in various stages of undress often enough that her heart had absolutely no excuse for beginning to beat so hard and fast. And yet he was so supremely male, so perfectly made, that she suspected that even given a lifetime of looking at him, her heart's clamouring reaction would never change.

'Let's go in for the first one,' he suggested. They moved into the sauna area, and the heat hit Shannie like a physical blow. Brand instructed her to lie down on the bottom bench while he climbed up into the heat of the top bench. The perspiration began to pour off Shannie almost instantly. She had a typical western aversion to sweat, and didn't think the experience was very sexy at all—until she glanced up at Brand.

His eyes were closed in contentment, his skin shining with beads of sweat—he looked rather like a body builder who had applied lotion to his body to make it glow magnificently, or like a statue cast in shining bronze.

'Enough for the first time,' he pronounced, just as she was sure her skin was melting to the bench. He led them out of the room, and then outside. She followed him hesitantly as he went and stood, face turned to the heavens, in the pouring rain. She followed his example and then smiled with delight. The physical sensation was exquisite—the cold, gentle rain hitting the hot surface of her skin, making it feel vibrant and tingly, as if it danced with a life of its own. And despite the sweat she felt remarkably refreshed, wonderfully clean.

They returned inside, sipped wine, listened to music, and then repeated the procedure—this time having a 'wet' sauna: pouring water on the hot rocks of the sauna to create steam, and then once again dashing out into the rain.

After the third sweat, by far the hottest, they burst outside. Brand dashed down the stone stairs that led to the creek and threw himself in. After only a moment's hesitation, Shannie followed him. She shrieked at the shock of the water, and then laughed with pure delight, feeling it rush coolly over her burning body. Brand came over and wrapped his arms around her, and they sat on the bottom of the creek, the water up to their necks singing by them. His embrace seemed completely natural—the warmth of his skin radiating through the water, dispelling some of its chill.

She lifted her face to the rain, and his eyes caught on her lips, and with a smile he touched his to hers. The kiss deepened and she turned more to him, needing the sensuous feel of his hard chest, of his wet, silky skin against hers.

With a sudden groan he picked her up, carried her back up the stairs, and into the scrub-room. Feeling languidly drugged by the pure physical sensuality of the experience she watched as he filled a large bucket, first with water boiling inside a container in the sauna, and then adding it to water that had to be hand-pumped from the creek. He tested it, then came to her, set the bucket down, and got one of the wooden dippers she had been admiring earlier. She closed her eyes as the water washed over her, and then he was massaging the soap into the silken surface of her skin with slow, circular movements, the strength those mighty hands were capable of carefully leashed. The creaminess of the soap added a texture to his touch that left her breathless.

She didn't know, finally, if it was the wine, or if she was drunk on the incomparable physical sensations being introduced to her by the whole experience. But she opened her eyes and looked at him, unaware of the burning intensity her gaze held. 'I think I'm ready to become a little more Finnish,' she murmured throatily, oddly unembarrassed by her boldness.

He looked less startled than concerned, and he scanned her face gently. 'Are you very sure, Shannie?'

She nodded, and he took her in his arms, and covered her face and throat with featherlight kisses, his questing lips moving ever downward, leaving a trail of fire in their wake. Then, with a touch so light she barely felt it, he lowered the straps of her bathing-suit, and she stepped out of it, standing before his burning eyes naked and proud—not in the least self-conscious or unsure.

'Shannie,' he whispered, the look in his eyes as they swept down her reinforcing her confidence, her absolute sense of rightness in what she had done. His eyes convinced her she was beautiful to him in a way that words could never have done.

And then he, too, was naked, and they stood exploring each other with wondering eyes. It struck her that this was man in his natural state—raw, unconstricted, totally and intensely beautiful. It was her last objective thought, for he reached once again for the soap and then they were lost within a misty dream of soap and sensuality, water and questing lips and worshipful touches.

'Shannie,' he whispered raggedly, pulling slightly away from her. His face was drawn, as if the act of lifting his lips from her skin had caused him pain. His eyes had turned to black and burned with a fierce fire of wanting. They conquered hers, demanding an answer.

She nodded, the question understood, and the conquerer became the captured. He buried his face in her neck, inhaling her scent with a reverence that should have been reserved only for the most beloved. And then slowly his lips anointed her neck, moving steadily, stealthily downward to the gentle curve of her breast.

She gasped, burned by an intensity more

powerful than anything she had ever known. She was being totally swept away—by his need of her, by her need of him. It was intoxicating, wonderful, joyous.

He once again lifted her into his arms, and then carried her naked, through the rain, to his van.

He opened the side door, and she found herself being placed on a soft bed, the smell of wonderfully clean sheets enveloping her. She reached for him with a hunger that astonished her, but in no way shamed her. Everything that had happened tonight had seemed right—like a natural conclusion to the tension that had been steadily building in her since Brand's arrival on her doorstep weeks ago.

Though there was urgency in his eyes, and in his ragged breathing, there was nothing urgent in the way his hands and lips claimed her. They played across her gently, and with infinite tenderness, his very control, the caring it reflected, arousing her to the point of no return, and driving her wild with wanting. But it seemed he was determined that his lips would taste every inch of her, and the soft coos and sighs of desire that breathed from her of their own volition did nothing to hasten him.

Her lips returned the interest of his, gently devouring him. She tasted the honey of his lips, the roughness of his cheekbones, the spice of his shoulders. She ran an inquisitive tongue over his hard nipples, and over the hair of his belly.

'Brand!' she finally cried softly, her voice an animal moan of pleasure and pleading.

His eyes were fastened on her face, smouldering with passion, and yet something gentler, too. He lowered himself on to her, saying her name over and over in a gentle, wondering, rasping whisper.

She opened to him, like a flower opening to the sun, her eyes never leaving his face. She was so glad that she had waited for him, so happy that she had waited for just the right person to share this so-special moment with.

'Shannie?' he said, with sudden surprise, the tempo of his body freezing, his face puzzled and then concerned, and then cherishing as if he knew she had saved this gentle gift just for him. 'Shannie,' he murmured at the look in her eyes, and then seeing what was in them, he smiled tenderly, and there was no turning back.

Afterwards, she felt deeply contented, wordless, wonderfully exhausted. Her first love-making had been painless and exquisite. The novels and the magazine articles that waxed poetic about this experience had missed something—had not been able to capture or articulate the full glory, the full rapture of a man and a woman together, forming these timeless bonds.

In some far reach of her gold gauze-shrouded mind was the awareness that they would need to talk. What had just passed between them was the final expression of all that came before, and there were so many dimensions of each other that needed to be explored with words as well as with caresses. But now was not the time for that. Now was the time for savouring, for languishing, for lingering in that physical expression of love that was so powerful, so magnificent, so intense. She sighed, his arm tightened around her. She planted a few sleepy, sated kisses in the general region of his face, gave a kitten-like mew, and fell asleep, secure in the circle of his arms. The rain continued to beat a soft tattoo on the roof.

CHAPTER NINE

SHANNIE stretched like a contented cat, and opened her eyes. At first she was slightly disconcerted to find herself in her own bed, but then she vaguely recalled Brand wrapping her naked body tenderly in his fluffy, feather-tick quilt, taking her from the van, and carrying her through the rain up the path. Nestled safe and warm against him, she had fallen instantly back to sleep.

She turned now, eager to greet him, to touch him, to awaken him with playful nips and kisses. She frowned in shock at the empty place beside her. Surely he had slept with her? The fear that he might have left her alone—that it might have meant so little to him—passed instantly. His side of the bed was thoroughly rumpled. And then her gaze went to his pillow. A note was pinned to it.

She unpinned it, relishing the feeling of delicious intimacy it gave her—delighting in the new-found discovery that love made something as tiny as a note pinned to a pillow wonderfully special and fun. For the first time in her life, she could claim membership in that exclusive club of twos, of pairs, and discover all the intimate and private rituals that were insinuated in the looks that passed between those hand-in-hand couples she had seen all her life.

She opened the note, and grinned. A stick-man was clicking his heels in a joyous jig, his face one huge smile. 'I think I'm in love with you,' the caption read. The postscript added that he'd gone for a morning run.

She sat smirking idiotically at the note for much longer than either the words or the dubious artwork warranted. Of course, she didn't quite know what to make of the *think*. A plain, 'I'm in love with you', might have been nicer. And she was a little unsettled at the thought that the note followed so quickly in the wake of their love-making. Did Brand, physical being that he was, mistake the physical act for love? Did he think that was all there was to it?

'Shannie, Shannie, Shannie,' she chided herself. Finally she folded the note carefully and put it in the drawer of her night table. Brand had obviously not spent three hours composing a love letter—it was just a spontaneous little note, not ever meant to be dissected mercilessly for hidden meanings, or deep psychological hold-outs. As for him falling in love as a result of last night— who was she kidding? She had been an inexperienced virgin, a fact that she rather doubted her very sincere ardour had disguised. If Brand were going to fall in love based on a performance in bed, it didn't seem likely he would choose her. Besides, she wasn't prepared to believe Brand would be shallow enough to base a declaration of love on a solely physical liaison. No, what had happened last night had been a joyous confirmation—a sealing of what hearts and minds had already discovered.

She made the surprised, somewhat delighted discovery that she didn't even resent the fact he'd gone jogging. It was based on the awareness—and the acceptance—of the fact that there were some things about them that were very, very different. It would be a mistake, she recognised with tranquil calm, to try and change those things—to ever insinuate she could love him better 'if' . . .

And with that awareness came her knowledge of just how deep her feelings went—just how real her love was. It wasn't a childhood crush returned to haunt her, it wasn't an infatuation, it wasn't an act of being 'star-struck'. Because she loved him so much just the way he was. She didn't feel he had to change to fit better her romantic ideals. She could even accept the fact that football owned part of him—which was quite a testimony to the strength of her feeling. He had gently taken down that barrier, eased the hurts that the miserable game had caused her, and shown her it wasn't so much the game, as the people who played it, and their attitude towards it. And he wasn't any of those people who had caused her past hurts. For the first time in her life she was capable of separating a football player from her father's pain, her mother's ambitions, her brothers' stardom, the loneliness and misunderstandings of her childhood. For the first time, she felt certain that when Brand said he thought

he loved her, he meant just that. He didn't mean
he wanted to get closer to her brothers, or bask in
their reflected glory. He didn't mean he really
wanted one more person to adore him. He didn't
mean he wanted to take and take and take, and
give nothing back.

Shannie glanced at the clock and wrinkled her
nose. No wonder Brand had gone jogging! The
morning person in him wouldn't tolerate very
many eleven o'clock risings. Nice, though—he
really didn't seem to mind it in her. Her smile
deepened. And she might as well enjoy it while
she could—once they started having a family, it
wasn't likely she'd be given many opportunities
to sleep in.

A family, she mused dreamily. Stocky little
babies with huge brown eyes who would run
whooping through this house, who would ride on
their daddy's broad shoulders . . .

For a moment she was aghast at herself. A note
with a cartoon on it was a pretty flimsy
declaration of love—so was a night of passion, for
that matter. And here she was, planning a family
around it! How right Brand had been when he
had seen her real motives for buying this house—
though how desperately she wanted that dream
took even her a bit by surprise.

And then there was the small chance that last
night might result in the beginnings of a family.
It occurred to her, with things so unsettled, with
so much unspoken between her and Brand, that
the very idea should terrorise her. God, her

mother's reaction alone——

And yet what she felt was not terror. She felt calm and strangely serene. A deep, deep trust in Brand shone through all that had not been said. Besides, he had claimed not very long ago that he just knew she couldn't ever hurt him, and she felt certain that he, too, was incapable of inflicting pain. Not on her, and not intentionally. Anyway, regardless of her circumstances, she just couldn't feel anything but good in connection with the thought of a little bundle of life nuzzled trustingly into her breast.

Languidly, aware of the subtlest of changes in the way she felt about herself and her body, Shannie got up and showered. While in the shower she decided to put on a special brunch for Brand and herself. It would be fun to discuss some of the things that needed discussing over orange juice and champagne, fresh croissants, a spinach quiche, and strawberries and cream. A few candles in the middle of the day might be fun, too. She laughed out loud. How glorious it felt to be in love! What an adventure it made of life! How each day, and every mundane little activity and detail seemed to hold a sparkle and a promise that it had never held before!

She realised she didn't have any of the ingredients for her brunch but, since Brand wasn't back yet anyway, she had time for a quick run into Salmon Arm. And if brunch was served at three, or six, or ten, who cared?

She left him a quick note, and barrelled into

Salmon Arm, recklessly ignoring posted speed limits for the first time in her life. She wanted to be back quickly ... to be with him, to throw herself wantonly into his arms and kiss his eyes, his nose, his lips—oh yes, his lips!

She went through the grocery store in a haze, regretting the fact that she hadn't made a list. It was very hard keeping her mind on ingredients for brunch when her mind had already skipped beyond brunch, to her wild cherry bed, and to the feel of his hands on her. She was sure her thoughts must be an open book to everyone she passed, since she was flushing wildly, and an eager, tender smile kept tugging at her lips.

Finally, she thought she had everything, and didn't really care if she did or not. She was considering maybe skipping the brunch and getting right to——

Her thoughts stopped dead. Everything stopped dead. The movement in the check-out line in front of her and the beat of her own heart were frozen as still as a black and white photo. Greta Mason's tear-stained face took up nearly the whole front cover of *Starline Express*, a weekly newspaper devoted to gossip about the celebrities, pseudo-celebrities, and out-and-out nuts. Usually Shannie only felt slightly amused disdain for the black headlines that leapt off the newsprint.

Now she felt faint. *HE'S DEAD* the bold headline shouted. It was followed by a stark subheading. *Greta fears worst for fiancé, Brand Heaton.*

'That'll be fifteen sixty-seven, miss.'

Shannie looked blankly at the cashier, then fumbled for her wallet. Numbly she added the *Express* to her purchases.

The cashier glanced at the headline with ghoulish interest. 'Do you suppose it's true?' she whispered mournfully.

'I guarantee you it wasn't true this morning,' Shannie informed her tightly, 'but it well might be by tonight.'

Ignoring the astonished glance of the cashier, she took her bag of groceries and marched out to her car. The door had barely crashed closed behind her when she began flipping roughly through the paper to locate the story. Considering the size of the picture of Greta and the headline the actual story was brief and hard to find.

'Greta Mason was near hysteria today when she announced to the Press that her fiancé, Brand Heaton, had been missing for a month. The beautiful, blonde actress now fears the worst. Mason, the star of the recently cancelled series *Dog Daze*, says she and Heaton became secretly engaged at Christmas time.

'"I loved him very much," the misty-eyed actress told reporters, "but after the Super Bowl injury he was a changed man. He knew his career was over. He became depressed, without hope. I was beside him all the time, despite the fact that my own work suffered because of my devotion to Brand. I feel the cancellation of my series was probably because I was very preoccupied. The suffering of my beloved was *my* suffering."'

'Oh, barf,' Shannie muttered.

"'But all my love wasn't enough. He just sank deeper and deeper into the pit of despair. Without his career, I think he felt his very masculinity was threatened, and what man can live without that? Though it frightens me to even speculate, I have to say now that I think the worst. Brand is— was—such a caring and gentle person underneath his public image. He could never be callous and insensitive enough to leave without a word, without contacting me."'

The article concluded with a brief paragraph describing Brand's career and the injury he'd received during the Super Bowl.

Shannie threw down the magazine in disgust. Greta Mason's least believable role was as a modern-day, self-sacrificing Florence Nightingale. Her insinuation that Brand's masculinity could ever be threatened by *anything* was outrageous. Her implication that he might kill himself was not only ridiculous but insulting in the extreme to Brand. It showed how well she herself knew the real man! A man who radiated such an intense love of life, a man whose confidence, whose terrific self-certainty and vitality made itself known in his every move— even if those movements were temporarily crippled—did not give up. He was a fighter, for

God's sake! Snakes would sprout wings before Brand even contemplated killing himself, of that Shannie was sure.

Brand depressed? Well, certainly Shannie had witnessed his mood swings, but nothing she had seen could be labelled even mild depression and nothing she had seen could make her agree with Greta's portrait of him as a pathetic invalid who would give up on life rather than never play football again.

Shannie pounded her fists against the steering wheel. What kind of nincompoop had Brand got himself hooked up with? Or was Greta another victim? Because, for all the rubbish that the article had carelessly spewed, there was a line of truth there that made Shannie uneasy about dismissing all of it. Greta was obviously close enough to Brand to have seen that gentle and caring side of him that was not on public view.

Or was he the grand actor? Was that 'gentle and caring' side the biggest lie of all? Used to suck them all in—Greta, the angel, herself? What was the real scoop on his relationship with the gorgeous blonde starlet? If he was engaged to her, who was the girl whose picture he kept in his room? Who called him in the middle of the night? Who was Kel? Shannie scowled ferociously.

Why had she ever allowed herself to be lulled by him, to dismiss what she had known were legitimate complications in his forming a relationship? Oh, Brand Heaton had some questions to answer, and it sure as hell wasn't going to be over candlelight and champagne and orange juice!

Unfortunately, his van was gone when she returned. She couldn't believe it. How dared he take off when she was angry enough to burst! When she needed to confront him immediately! When she needed to yell and scream, and rant and accuse!

He had tacked a few short lines on to the note she had left for him in the breakfast nook.

'Dear Shannaleigh'—she did not smile at his attempt to guess her name—'something urgent has come up. I'll have to be gone for a few days. My apologies for the bad timing. I'll call tonight, Love, Brand.'

She slammed the note back on to the table. Had news of his demise reached him by radio—or by that television he kept in his room? He hadn't hesitated to sign with love, she noticed grimly, but then maybe he signed his notes to *all* his lovers with love. Oh, he'd been appropriately named. He had more irons in the fire than he was going to be able to handle!

Suddenly the anger drained out of her. She sat down at the breakfast nook, nestled her hands in her arms and cried. How could he do this to her? And how could she be fool enough to be deceived by him? To be taken in by all that well practised, slick charm and charisma?

In her mind she had convicted him as a cold-hearted arch villian so many times that afternoon that she was very surprised when the phone actually did ring that night. She stared at it vindictively. Let him think it meant as little to her as it had to him! Let him think that she was out laughing and having fun with somebody else tonight. Let him——

Oh, hell, it probably wasn't even him. She sighed and picked up the phone—and was forced to admit that in her deepest heart she hoped it was him, after all.

'Shannie? Brand.' His voice was a long way away, the line hissed with static and his words faded in and out. Still, she had to fight to bring her outlaw heart under control. '——longer note, but I had to make the flight connection out of Kamloops, or wait until tomorrow ... damn, is this line as bad at your end as mine? ... Shannie, I have so much to say to you, but I'm standing in a corridor and this blasted line ... will you wait till I get back? ... don't know when ... it looks like it's nearly the ...'

Had the line faded or had his voice suddenly thickened with emotion? Some instinct told her there was something wrong, that he was caught, again, in some web of suffering. Some instinct begged her to trust him and wait until he returned to confront him, to hear him out——

But that instinct warred with the part of her that had spent the better part of the day feeling betrayed and gullible and angry. That instinct warred with the part of her that thought Brand might be playing her for a fool, using her as a sucker.

'Were the rumours of your death greatly exaggerated?' she shouted, borrowing a line from Mark Twain.

'What? Shannie, I can hardly hear you. There's a storm here that must be interfering with the reception. Look, I'll try and call you tomorrow . . . I love you.'

Now she felt bitterly certain he had heard her perfectly, and was buying the time by putting her off with soft words. The anger, now that she'd allowed it to surface, continued to bubble inside her and flow out.

'How's Greta?' she asked sharply, refusing to let him off the hook that easily.

'Greta? *Greta Mason?* How the hell would I know?'

There was a note of impatience in his voice that enraged her further. He couldn't wait to hang up the phone, and be rid of her! Well, to hell with him!

'You know, Greta Mason, your fiancée?' It was hard to sound sweet when you had to shout, but she still tried.

Several choice swear words reached her.

'It's illegal to use profanity on the phone,' she informed him primly.

'I don't give a damn! What are you talking about, Shannie?' His voice was coming across the lines much clearer now that it was a bellow.

'I'm talking about the cover story in the

Starline Express this morning—Greta Mason proclaiming to the world that her fiancé—namely you—had most likely committed suicide.'

'The *Express*? For God's sake, Shannie, they print exclusive interviews with aliens from the planet Venus, and have scooped the second coming at least three times!' The static suddenly left the line, and his voice came as clearly as though he were standing at her ear. 'Shannie, couldn't you trust me just a little more than that?' His voice was suddenly low and disappointed, as if he were a million miles from home, and she had made him sadder and lonelier than he already was.

She felt an overwhelming wave of guilt—followed by a wave of fresh anger. He was manipulating her to feel guilty—when so far all the evidence was stacked against *him*.

'Well, even if there's nothing between you and Greta, who's the woman in the picture you keep in your room?'

There was a long silence. His voice, when he spoke, was like gravel. 'Her name's Kelly O'Rourke.' And then, as it had done once before, his voice thickened, and this time there was no mistaking it for static. It was emotion. 'I have to go.' Without saying goodbye, he hung up the phone.

Shannie stared at the dead phone, stricken. Intuitively she knew she had made a mistake—knew she should have heeded that quiet voice within that had begged her to trust him.

She didn't even have a number where she could reach him—reach him and explain how she was new to this love stuff—and how she didn't quite trust it or herself. She desperately wanted to tell him how she couldn't quite bring herself to believe something so wonderful could happen to Shannie Smith—and last. She wanted to share with him that she had never been in love, and it seemed a fragile thing—how could anything so beautiful not shatter into a million pieces at the touch of a human hand? And maybe it was fragile. Maybe she had just wrecked everything in a few seconds on the telephone.

Snuggles crawled up on the couch beside her. The dog was not allowed on the furniture, and yet he was steadfastly determined to put his duty to his mistress before the rules. She gave him a half-hearted shove. His bulk became immovable, and tentatively he reached out his pink, rough tongue and licked the tears from her cheek. Then, with a sigh of infinite understanding, Snuggles laid his heavy head on her breast and closed his eyes. Ignoring the fact that he was slobbering profusely, Shannie wrapped her arms around him and hugged him tightly. Fresh tears gathered in her eyes and slipped down her cheeks. Was this what the rest of her life was going to be like? Her and a dog? Much as she loved her dog, it was a dreary and cheerless prospect.

Once, before she had known any differently, that life had seemed like enough. She had even been proud of the fact that she had attained such independence, such total self-reliance. Now she saw her former life-style for what it was—a philosophical victory. Because Brand had shown her a dimension that no life should be without. A healthy dimension—she didn't *need* him to support her, to make her feel secure, to look after her. No, she had already proven she could do all that herself. She *wanted* Brand. To add a quality of laughter and sparkle to her life, to enrich and enhance it. That was different from needing, in the most important of ways.

It had been important for her to learn to stand alone—to be capable of independence and self-sufficiency—but it was also important to learn to exist within relationships. The first led to the second—didn't exclude it. A relationship should be a blending of two strong, rich flavours—not one swallowing the other—but each adding to what the other had been, making it something better than it was before.

And that's what she and Brand did for one another—made better, stronger, richer. They blended outlooks, viewpoints, and strong, independent personalities into a sparkling and vibrant wellspring of life.

One fight, one misunderstanding, couldn't change all that, could it? No, not if it was what she thought it was. And if it wasn't—if it was just an illusion—it wasn't worth having, anyway.

Suddenly she felt confident. Brand would get over being angry and hurt. He would take some time and think about it from her viewpoint and he would understand. He'd call, and he would explain who Kelly O'Rourke was, and they'd both laugh at the relationship that her over-worked imagination had placed him in. There would be an explanation for that photo on his dresser—just as there had been an explanation for Greta Mason.

There was only one problem with Shannie's little theory. A week passed, and Brand didn't call—and with each passing day, her confidence died another agonising inch.

She went back to 'their' beach, a little horrified by her masochistic tendency towards self-torture. Still, she couldn't stop herself. There were small pieces of him there, just as there were small pieces of him around the house—and she felt driven to collect up these tiny, broken fragments and glue them back together in her mind.

She was strolling back up the lane, her head down, her heart lingering on the beach and in the past, when she looked up and her breath caught in her throat. Yes, there was a little grey showing over the top of her hedge! Could it be? She began to walk faster, afraid to get her hopes up. But it was! It was his van! He was back! She broke into a run, laughter starting to bubble again inside her, life ebbing back into the deadness of her soul.

'Brand?' she called breathlessly from the hall. There was no answer, but she could hear him moving about in his room. She took the stairs two at a time, and burst in on him without knocking,

uncaring that her joy shone in her face like a
beacon.

For a moment she felt only puzzled, and then
the joy fizzled like a firework that had got wet,
that had started to explode, but never quite made
it.

The crushing sense of despondency was back,
more intense than it had ever been. At least before
things had seemed up in the air—it had seemed
like there was a chance—that maybe he would
come back, that maybe they would patch thing;
up, that maybe there was a reason for his week
long silence. Now, watching him unhitch his
equipment, she faced the truth. Shannie Smith
had never really had a chance with Brand Heaton.
He was moving on, leaving. She never thought
seeing the torture chamber dismantled would be
the thing that would break her heart—but life
was full of these cruel ironies.

She slumped on to his bed. He didn't even
acknowledge her presence. His back was to her,
and she dimly noticed that he was ripping apart
his equipment with an energy that sizzled with
anger. Her eyes moved to the dresser. The picture
still sat there, smiling that strange, wise Mona
Lisa smile.

'So, it's over,' Shannie said softly, the words
forced in a hideous attempt at conversation, at
pretending there was nothing wrong in her
world.

The wrench paused in its feverish motion, and
Brand became very still. The wrench dropped

from a lifeless hand.

'Yes, it's over,' he confirmed tonelessly, those massive shoulders slumped, his proud head sagging.

She got up. It was evident from his stature that those words were painful to him. So, it hurt him a bit, too. Who could say? That might be a source of great comfort to her in her old age, when she relived these moments, these weeks. That it had hurt him, too.

She walked stiffly to the door, fighting the impulse to beg him for a chance to explain her jealousies, to ask what had happened, why he had gone, why he wouldn't give her—them—another opportunity. But she was determined to save this last shred of dignity. She would not beg him to stay. Besides, she had no guarantee that it would be words that would come out of her mouth. It might be a wail of pure and desperate despair like the cry of an animal trapped in a corner, caught in a trap. And she was caught—in the trap of her own treacherous heart.

Her hand was on the doorknob when the sharp sound of glass shattering halted her. She turned slowly back. Brand was facing her now, but not looking at her. He was looking down at the floor, fury in every line of his face.

Her eyes shifted to the dresser, as if she couldn't believe what she had seen on the floor. But no, the place where that picture had stood a moment ago was empty. Her eyes drifted back to the floor. The picture was face down in a wreckage of splintered glass.

Slowly, she looked at Brand. The fury had faded, and was replaced by a despair so deep she could not stop herself. She loved him, and she could not walk away from his pain. She loved him, and some code of honour deep within her insisted that she comfort him, even if there was nothing in it for her ...

She went to him, wrapped her arms around him, placed her head against his breast. For a moment he stood stiff in her arms, and then he was rocked by a great tremor, and his arms closed around her desperately, as if he needed the warmth of her body, needed to feel her life-blood flowing through her.

She could feel tremendous shudders continue to rack him, and when she felt his tears wash down her neck, she began to cry too, his mysterious pain becoming hers, filling her with an aching sadness.

'She died, Shannie,' he whispered, his voice so choked at first she couldn't quite understand him. And then she did—the beautiful young woman in the photograph was dead.

'I did everything I knew how,' he whispered helplessly. 'And she still died, Shannie. It's over. It's over.'

CHAPTER TEN

AFTER an endless moment, Brand drew away from her. 'Shannie, give me a few minutes by myself,' he asked, turning his back to her. His typical masculine shame in openly displaying his emotions was evident in the sudden shuttering of his features. 'I'll come downstairs in a few minutes and we can talk.'

'All right.' She hesitated. 'Brand, it takes a man to admit life has hurt him. Only boys run away from their tears.'

He turned and looked at her sombrely, then gave her a weary smile. 'Thanks,' he said softly, and turned back to the window.

She was perking coffee and warming biscuits when he joined her in the kitchen. He settled himself at the breakfast nook. Silently she brought over the pot, two mugs and a plate of hot biscuits. She sat down across from him, taking in his tired face with compassion. She noticed how haggard he looked—grey shadows under his eyes, a few days' growth of beard darkening his hollowed cheeks. Still, there was a calmness in his expression that had been missing before.

'I'm sorry I subjected you to that,' he apologised quietly. 'It's been a tough week.' His eyes held hers, and then his hand inched across the table, seeking hers. He sighed with weary contentment when her hand reached out to meet his, and then was folded firmly within his palm.

'I wanted to call you a hundred times this week,' he confessed haltingly. 'I needed you. I needed so badly to hear your voice. But I couldn't trust myself to speak—I was scared I'd start to talk and all the rage and confusion I was feeling would just come screaming out of me. That wouldn't have been fair to you, because you didn't know what was happening at my end.' His eyes clouded, and his voice roughened. 'She was only sixteen, Shannie.'

She felt no reaction of alarm or horror. From the very tone of his voice she knew that everything she'd ever assumed about his relationship to the young woman, 'the angel' in that photograph, had been wrong. The only thing she'd got right was sensing the youth and innocence. Now, she had a feeling she was going to find out the secret behind the expression in those ageless eyes.

'I met her in the hospital after I got hurt. What a kid!' A smile of fond remembrance lit his dark eyes. 'She knew every statistic, every team in the league, every player. I was her favourite. She'd come every day, bounce into my room, sit on my bed in an enormous hot-pink housecoat. At first I think I was just polite to her. I had my own troubles. Hell, I was hurting. But at some point I really started to look forward to her little visits. She could make me forget for a while that I was in pain. Hospitals are dull and gloomy places, and she was irrepressible, and bubbling with life—a

little beam of sunshine to brighten up my dreary
days.

'Anyway, after a couple of weeks of chatting
about football and our mutual heroes, we started
to get a little more personal. That's when I found
out she didn't have tonsillitis or appendicitis or
whatever it is that kids go to the hospital for.
That's when I found out she had cancer.

'I've never felt such rage or helplessness in my
whole life—except maybe again last week. This
beautiful little girl was going to die before she
lived.' He was silent for a long time.

'Anyway, I guess it was because I did feel so
helpless that I made the deal with her. You see, I
talked to one of the doctors about her condition,
and he said she could go any time—or be around
for a few more years. I asked him what made the
difference, and he didn't know. Certainly drug
treatments and stuff helped, but he said he
thought the single most important factor was
hope. And he said kids got attached to the
weirdest hopes—a new kitten or a promised trip
to Disneyland might keep them alive longer than
anybody expected.

'So , anyway, one day she's sitting on my bed,
chattering away like any sixteen-year-old, and
then suddenly she got serious. "When are you
going to play football again, Brand?" So I told
her what I was just beginning to accept—that it
was quite likely I'd never play ball again. "Oh,"
she said. And then she looked at me with just a
touch of mischief glowing in those big eyes, and
said she supposed if a big, tough guy like me

could quit, it would be OK for her to quit, too. That's when we made the deal—I promised her I'd play again, and she promised she'd be around to see me.'

He sighed, 'And that's where it started to get a little crazy in my head. I *knew* it was crazy, but I couldn't stop myself. Somehow I figured it was true—like I'd made a bargain with fate. That if I could play again, she could live. It was like all my life, Shannie, I've come up against formidable opponents and won, so I was searching for the rules, the game plan to help me win against death. What good was any of it, if you couldn't save one little girl? In the beginning, I just thought I was giving her something to hope for and hold on to— she was really sick that first time we met. But then when she had her remission, I started to believe it. I started to believe that maybe, in some way I couldn't understand, I was partly responsible for her getting better. That's when I came out here— I was going to do nothing but work to get that leg in shape—to play ball again for Kelly. And then Trish—her mom—phoned and told me she'd relapsed, and I nearly went crazy with guilt. I'd been spending my time with you, I'd been backsliding on my resolve. I wasn't only not sure if I would play football again, I wasn't even sure I wanted to. It felt like a good time to let it go—to start looking at a new life.' He looked intently at Shannie, and her heart leapt. She had not a doubt that his thoughts of a new life were inspired by her and included her.

'But I owed her first,' he continued softly,

'before I could even think about it. I'd made a deal—and I took it seriously. I lost. Holding the line against death just isn't the same ball game. But it hurts, Shannie. It's the first time in my life that I haven't been able to do something I set my mind to doing—and, in retrospect, it was the only time it was important.'

'Oh, Brand,' she said softly, almost bursting with pride and joy for the giant heart inside that broken body, 'don't you see it doesn't matter? You don't win or lose against destiny. You just go with it. All that matters is that you came to know each other. I'm sure it gave Kelly a great deal of joy to know you, and to know how much you cared about her.'

He smiled. 'I want you to understand this about Kelly—she always gave more than she took. Even in the end, her first concern seemed to be helping everybody else to cope. And, even though she was in immense pain, she had somehow guessed there was something or somebody new in my life and she insisted on hearing all about you.

'It was very close to the end when she said, "Brand, if it weren't for me, you would have never met Shannie, would you?" And it was true. I wouldn't have been looking for a place to escape from the Press, a place to work out without distractions, if it hadn't been for my personal Holy Grail. And then she smiled, and said, "I'll be gone, but do you suppose what's best about me will go on, Brand? Do you suppose the joy and love lives on, maybe through you and Shannie?"'

He brushed gently at the tears that coursed down Shannie's face. 'I told her, yeah, I supposed it did.' He paused. 'What do you think, Shannie?'

Shannie just shook her head, too choked to speak. She was remembering the mystery in that girl—that look of wisdom, of tranquillity. She hadn't quite been able to place it, but now she knew what it had been. Love. Pure love. Yes, the best part of Kelly O'Rourke lived on.

Brand stood up, and she went weeping into his arms. But somewhere along the way the tears had changed from sadness for a girl she didn't know and would never have the opportunity to meet. Somewhere along the way the tears had changed to joy.

'Well, when are we going to get married?'

They were lying side by side at the beach, both turning golden brown, their hands intertwined.

'Brand Heaton!' She tried for indignation, but somehow the lazily contented note never left her voice. 'That was a shabby and lack-lustre proposal,' she informed him primly.

He closed his eyes. 'Just testing the water. I don't want to lay my heart at your feet just to have it walked on. I mean, maybe you think it's crazy. We haven't known each other that long. Maybe it's only me feeling so good and so special.' He sighed melodramatically. 'It's quite possible you've just been toying with my heart.'

She took her hand from his, brushed gently at the wayward strands of silver-streaked hair falling over his eyes. The small intimacy sent a thrill of wonder through her, and she studied his face tenderly. Little by little, the lop-sided grins and the small jokes had been slipping through the wall of his sorrow. Now, after three weeks, he seemed to have made a complete recovery from his grief—or as complete a recovery as could be expected of the human heart.

He had quietly and wordlessly dismantled his gym and taken it piece by piece to the cellar. And, despite the fact he was in a state of unspoken mourning, a quiet time of wonder and discovery had begun to unfold for both of them.

Shannie was still startled at how easily he fitted into her life-style. She had always considered herself to be somewhat of a loner. On those rare occasions when she had contemplated marriage, she had despaired at ever finding someone who would be able to put up with her moods and messes, who would be able to respect her need for quiet time and privacy. And yet all she felt, sharing her life with Brand, was a shivering sensation of well-being as he moved closer and closer to her.

They had been working together on the gable-room for the past few weeks. Without asking, he'd just been there, giving the project an enthusiasm that easily matched her own. They pored over magazines together, pooled their knowledge, mulled over various ideas. Conversation between them was stimulating, laughter abundant, quiet times comfortable.

The days began to take on a pattern. Brand ran first thing in the morning. It was the only exercise he still did, and he explained to her his motivation wasn't to play football again, but to feel fit and to keep himself from going to fat. He shared with her his feelings about physical activity. He loved it in a way some people loved gardening or playing cards. The way she loved fixing up her old house. But his love of sport was a private one, and he never tried to convince her to join him—to her heartfelt relief.

When he had finished running, he would come home and cook breakfast, then wake her up to join him. While the house was still cool in the mornings they'd work on the gable-room. In the heat of the afternoon they would head for the beach, usually with a picnic lunch. They cooked dinners together, took Snuggles for ambling twilight walks down quiet country lanes, and finished the day cuddled up together on the sofa, listening to music, and sipping wine.

And somehow he slipped into her bed and her waiting arms just as easily and naturally as he had slipped into the rest of her life. Their exploration of each other, and their sense of discovery and wonder grew.

In the back of her mind it had occurred to her, once or twice, that this was not the kind of relationship her mother had intended or would have approved of when she was busily and deviously acting as matchmaker to Shannie and Brand. But then, it was not the kind of relationship she had ever pictured herself in, either. She had always been rather staunchly conservative when it came to moral values, as much as she was a bohemian in other respects. But now here she was, living with the man who was her lover, and unable to bring herself to care if she was thwarting convention or not.

What she and Brand had was right and good. It seemed as if it always had been and always would be. She felt no need to nail Brand down—to try and bind him to her—with a promise of for ever.

And yet now that he was holding out that golden promise of for ever to her she felt an incredible swelling of joy. Each day in his company had seemed enough—such a wonderful gift from life. She had not tempted the fates by asking for more. And now that he was offering more she felt an almost giddy sensation of having too much—too much love, too much happiness. What could she have done to have deserved this? She laughed out loud. He was asking her to share her whole life with him ... to wake up each morning in the circle of his arms ... to laugh with him ... to love him ... to have his children. She felt light-headed with joy, as effervescent as a champagne bubble, as buoyant as a balloon.

Brand's eyes re-opened. 'Quit chortling away to yourself and answer the question, wench,' he demanded. The look in his eyes belied his light, uncaring tone.

Shannie sighed with feigned heaviness. 'I could never marry anybody who called me a wench,' she teased.

He sighed, too, and reclosed his eyes. Shannie suppressed a giggle, though not the small smile that played across her lips. His face was completely relaxed, and she now knew Brand could go to sleep with catlike swiftness. Lulled into a sense of security, she rolled over on to her side.

'I guess this calls for harsher measures,' he growled into her ear. Before she had a chance to twist away, she found herself being lifted in powerful arms. Brand marched to the water's edge, unheeding of her squeals of outrage and her attempts to squirm free of his iron embrace. He continued unhesitatingly into the cold water until it rose to his waist and lapped with merry threat at her toes.

'Well?' he demanded, his laughing eyes on her face claiming her for ever as his own.

'Is there no romance in that brutish soul?' she asked sulkily. She clung to him tightly. 'I mean, couldn't you get down on one knee——'

He immediately complied, soaking them both thoroughly.

'Let me up! This water is damned cold! Brand Heaton——'

'Just answer the question,' he requested drily.

A peal of laughter escaped her lips, despite her attempts to remain sour-faced. 'What was it again?'

'It was "what does Shannie stand for?"'

'You cad!' She thumped him emphatically on the chest. 'That wasn't the question. It was——'

'Oh, Shannie! The answer to *that* question was in your eyes the whole time.'

She snuggled into his chest, her struggle forgotten. 'You're right. I love you, Brand, with all my heart and soul. I never expected to feel this wonderful about anybody in my whole life and——'

He poked a playful finger in her ribs. 'Quit trying to change the subject,' he warned sternly. 'If you don't tell me right now what Shannie stands for, it's under you go.'

'Bzzmfgkzzzllkk,' she mumbled unco-operatively.

'I didn't hear you.' He lowered her a bit more into the biting chill of the water.

'OK! OK!' She lowered her voice until it was almost inaudible. 'It's Shenendoah.'

He kissed her and lifted her out of the water. 'I feel cheated. Why wouldn't you want to tell me that? It think it's a beautiful name. It suits you— it sounds as soft as a whispering breeze, and yet it's faintly wild, too. Did your parents fall in love with the Shenendoah Valley or something?' He carried her out of the water and set her down gently on the shore.

'I doubt my parents have ever seen the Shenendoah Valley. It's actually an Indian word—I don't know which nation—and it means something ludicrously romantic like "daughter of the stars". I always hated it. It was so different. But my mother always was determined all her children would be famous. She thought Smith was rather forgettable, so she did her best to help us along by making our first names something memorable. Len's real name is Leonardo, and Ray's is Beauregard. Thank God, my father undid the damage as much as possible by christening us all with nicknames as soon as we were brought home from the hospital.'

He seemed to recognise she was babbling, but waited patiently for her to stop. Finally, she wound down, and looked at him with wide eyes.

He touched his lips to hers. 'I think "daughter of the stars" is perfect for you, Shannie. Now, do you think you can be quiet for a minute?'

The kidding was over and the moment of truth had arrived. She did feel inexplicably nervous, but she nodded.

Brand dropped solemnly to one knee, took her hand, touched his lips to it. 'Shenendoah Smith, will you be my wife?'

She stared down at him, drinking in the way the sun glinted off his silver-tipped hair and his bronze-toned shoulders, drinking in the look in his eyes so she would remember this precious moment for all time. Her eyes clouded with tears and her voice shook. For the first time in her life, Shannie's name did not strike her as being entirely preposterous. Had not the universe, after all, bestowed upon her its greatest gift—the gift of love?

'Yes.'

He rose and gathered her into his arms. His lips dropped on to hers and she felt that now familiar thrill blaze through her veins. It was a lengthy kiss, and the sealing of their pact left them both breathless and longing for the future together.

'Shannie, I'd like your house to be our home base. I know what the inn means to you. Are you sure you're ready to share it?'

'Brand, the minute you walked in the door it

ceased to be *my* inn, and became an inn for two.'

'And some day, maybe, for three?' he asked huskily.

At first she didn't get his drift, but when she did she beamed at him. 'Yes,' she confirmed softly, a dark-eyed child already chortling and clapping chubby hands in some far off place in her mind.

'And then maybe for four?'

'Hmmmm,' she agreed dreamily.

'How about five?'

She frowned. 'Of course, you mean including Snuggles?'

'Of course, I *do not* mean including Snuggles,' he retorted indignantly.

'Oh! Then I think you're pushing your luck, Brand. I'm a career woman, after all.' But yes, five would be all right she decided inwardly. In fact, five would be perfect.

'Don't think I haven't noticed you looking at the accumulating *Kids' Corner* mail with love in your eyes,' he teased, and then became serious. 'Shannie, I would never expect you to give up being who you are because you happen to get married and start raising a family. I *want* to pull my weight as a parent. I want to be right in there—changing nappies and reading stories and juggling bottles. That's why I could never consider marriage and football at the same time. And if it becomes too much for us—even with me trying to be helpful, we'll get a nanny, or a housekeeper or whatever it takes. OK?'

'In that case, maybe we should go for an even

half-dozen.' She smiled up at him.

'Maybe an even dozen.'

'Brand!'

'OK, I'll behave myself.' He gave her a wolfish grin. 'Right after we pass the half-dozen mark.' He suddenly noticed how far the shadows had stretched out across the water. He reached for her, and hand in hand they began to walk home.

'I guess you have to arrange for a dress and invitations and all that.' He was trying to sound supportive, and instead sounded miserably impatient.

She laughed at his expression. 'No. I don't want any of that—I don't feel I need it. At the risk of sounding irreverent, I always thought large weddings were a little too much like the stage set for a Broadway extravaganza. No, I'd find it far more meaningful and real if this were just between you and me and the local Justice of the Peace.' She laughed again, this time devilishly. 'I'll break the news to my mother some time before the first child is born.'

'You do realise exactly what you're letting yourself in for, don't you?' he asked with sudden trepidation, his hand tightening on hers. 'I mean, there are probably always going to be Greta Masons in my life—people who are going to find it irresistible to try and use my name to further themselves or to prop up failing careers. You'd have to be prepared for that and worse, Shannie. Last year I was named in a paternity suit by a woman I had never even met. It's hard, Shannie, and sometimes it's going to require almost superhuman trust on your part. It'll take a while for the limelight to die, especially if——'

'Especially if?' she prodded, trying to fight the panic in her throat. What if he'd decided to go back to football, after all? What if she was going to have to share him with the game? Then, as suddenly as the fear had risen up in her, it was gone, and she wasn't afraid. She did trust. That fear belonged to a different set of circumstances—a different life. If he wanted to play football, all the more power to him. He was willing to support her in her career, and the least she could do for him was the same—support him in whatever he tried to do. She owed him a fresh slate.

'I've been asked to be a spokesperson for the Cancer Society. I wanted to talk it over with you before I accepted. You see, it would mean a fair bit of travelling. I'd be doing a lot of speaking engagements so it would also mean quite an investment of time and effort. It doesn't pay anything, and though money isn't going to be a concern, I want to know if you'd respect me if I just did volunteer labour for a year or two.'

'Respect you?' she repeated incredulously. 'Brand, I'd damned near revere you if you dedicated a year or two of your life to such a worthwhile cause.'

'Really?' He looked at her with tender and loving eyes. 'Oh, Shannie, you can't begin to know what that means to me.'

'It's important to me, too, Brand.' And then she knew how right she had been to be willing to trust him. He had never once used his fame for personal gain, but now he was going to unhesitatingly expose himself to that cruel and curious public eye for a cause he believed in.

Quite a man, she thought with wonder. And then, over the rise, she caught sight of the gabled roof of her house. His house. Their house. An inn for just two—for a little while longer, anyway.

ATTRACTIVE, SPACE SAVING BOOK RACK

Display your most prized novels on this handsome and sturdy book rack. The hand-rubbed walnut finish will blend into your library decor with quiet elegance, providing a practical organizer for your favorite hard-or soft-covered books.

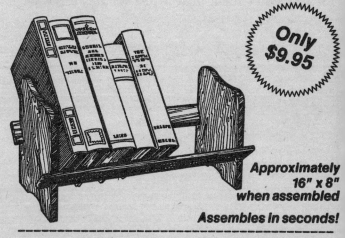

Only $9.95

Approximately 16" x 8" when assembled

Assembles in seconds!

To order, rush your name, address and zip code, along with a check or money order for $10.70* ($9.95 plus 75¢ postage and handling) payable to *Harlequin Reader Service*:

Harlequin Reader Service
Book Rack Offer
901 Fuhrmann Blvd.
P.O. Box 1396
Buffalo, NY 14269-1396

Offer not available in Canada.

BKR-1A

*New York and Iowa residents add appropriate sales tax.

Can you keep a secret?

You can keep this one plus 4 free novels

GIFTS FROM THE HEART

MAIL-IN-OFFER
OFFER CERTIFICATE ✂

I have enclosed the required number of proofs of purchase from any specially marked "Gifts From The Heart" Harlequin romance book, plus cash register receipts and a check or money order payable to Harlequin Gifts From The Heart Offer, to cover postage and handling.

002

CHECK ONE	ITEM	# OF PROOFS OF PURCHASE	POSTAGE & HANDLING FEE
	01 Brass Picture Frame	2	$ 1.00
	02 Heart-Shaped Candle Holders with Candles	3	$ 1.00
	03 Heart-Shaped Keepsake Box	4	$ 1.00
	04 Gold-Plated Heart Pendant	5	$ 1.00
	05 Collectors' Doll Limited quantities available	12	$ 2.75

NAME _____

STREET ADDRESS _____ APT. # _____

CITY _____ STATE _____ ZIP _____

Mail this certificate, designated number of proofs of purchase (inside back page) and check or money order for postage and handling to:

Gifts From The Heart, P.O. Box 4814
Reidsville, N. Carolina 27322-4814

NOTE THIS IMPORTANT OFFER'S TERMS

Requests must be postmarked by May 31, 1988. Only proofs of purchase from specially marked "Gifts From The Heart" Harlequin books will be accepted. This certificate plus cash register receipts and a check or money order to cover postage and handling must accompany your request and may not be reproduced in any manner. Offer void where prohibited, taxed or restricted by law. LIMIT ONE REQUEST PER NAME, FAMILY, GROUP, ORGANIZATION OR ADDRESS. Please allow up to 8 weeks after receipt of order for shipment. Offer only good in the U.S.A. Hurry—Limited quantities of collectors' doll available. Collectors' dolls will be mailed to first 15,000 qualifying submitters. All other submitters will receive 12 free previously unpublished Harlequin books and a postage & handling refund.

OFFER-1RR

PAMELA BROWNING

. . . is fireworks on the green at the Fourth of
July and prayers said around the
Thanksgiving table. It is the dream of
freedom realized in thousands of small
towns across this great nation.

But mostly, the Heartland is its people.
People who care about and help one another.
People who cherish traditional values and
give to their children the greatest gift, the
gift of love.

American Romance presents HEARTLAND,
an emotional trilogy about people whose
memories, hopes and dreams are bound up
in the acres they farm.

HEARTLAND . . . the story of America.

Don't miss these heartfelt stories: American
Romance #237 SIMPLE GIFTS (March),
#241 FLY AWAY (April), and
#245 HARVEST HOME (May).

HRT-1

GIFTS FROM THE HEART

from *Harlequin*

FREE BY MAIL

With proofs of purchase plus postage and handling

A. Hand-polished solid brass picture frame 1-5/8″ × 1-3/8″ with 2 proofs of purchase.

B. Individually handworked, pair of heart-shaped glass candle holders (2″ diameter), 6″ candles included, with 3 proofs of purchase.

C. Heart-shaped porcelain keepsake box (1″ high) with delicate flower motif with 4 proofs of purchase.

D. Radiant gold-plated heart pendant on 16″ chain with complimentary satin pouch with 5 proofs of purchase.

E. Beautiful collectors' doll with genuine porcelain face, hands and feet, and a charming heart appliqué on dress with 12 proofs of purchase. Limited quantities available. See offer terms.

HERE IS HOW TO GET YOUR FREE GIFTS

Send us the required number of proofs of purchase (below) of specially marked "Gifts From The Heart" Harlequin books and cash register receipts with the Offer Certificate (available in the back pages) properly completed, plus a check or money order (do not send cash) payable to Harlequin Gifts From The Heart Offer. We'll RUSH you your specified gift. Hurry—Limited quantities of collectors' doll available. See offer terms.

203R

GIFTS FROM THE HEART

ONE PROOF OF PURCHASE

To collect your free gift by mail you must include the necessary number of proofs of purchase with order certificate.